WARRIORS SHE KNEW

(Katie Parker Book 5)

CR HIATT

AMB

Leslie,
I hope you enjoy!
CR Hiatt

TABLE OF CONTENTS

AUTHOR'S NOTE

For entertainment purposes, I took certain liberties regarding certain law enforcement procedures. The town of Whispering Oak is a name I created for this story, but the town I used for the basis of the story actually exists.

<u>DEDICATION</u>

Dedicated to all the warriors out there…

PROLOGUE

FRANK MACINNIS—KNOWN as Mackie to the Veterans he served with and residents in the small town where he lived most of his adult life—eased out of bed and started his morning routine. Grunts and groans blessed his ears as he stretched his achy joints. At his age, some days were harder than others to get moving. It was Monday, so he pulled the comforter, blankets, and sheets off the bed, and strode across the cold hardwood floor to load them into the industrial-sized washer and dryer combo in the utility room just down the hall. His wife had been gone for a few years now, after dying from breast cancer, but he maintained the same chore schedule she had when she was alive. Washing the bedding each week was one discipline she brought into their young marriage before he shipped off to war all those years ago, and one he religiously continued. The only change was; he didn't bother separating the sheets from the bedspread to wash them in different loads, as his Rosie always instructed.

He set the machine so that it automatically switched to dry after the washing cycle and added fabric softener. Then he returned to his bedroom, grabbed the clothing he set out the night before, and headed into the bathroom to take a hot shower. It was still dark out, but he wanted to be at the Whispering Oak Diner the minute it opened, just as he had done for the last two decades. After his wife's passing, he continued to visit their favorite spot. Aside from the fact that they made an excellent omelet and ground their own beans with his favorite coffee flavor, he made it a point to always select the same booth, even though there was enough room for a family of six.

It was in the back corner, next to the window, that offered a view of the Chestnut Falls River. Rosie's favorite time to visit the cafe was during fall, when she could see the multi-colored leaves and foliage on the trees and bushes that lined both sides of the river, and continued up into the mountains. This was the time of year he enjoyed. At his age, the body ached more during the cold temperatures of winter, but the bare trees gave him a picturesque view of the gristmill waterfall after the old mill that was renovated into a bookstore and cafe.

Twenty minutes later, he was showered, shaved, and dressed in the usual attire that made him resemble a lumberjack in a logging town, or as Rosie used to tease: Elmer Fudd. He left his bedroom and glanced toward the Grandfather clock when he entered his favorite room in the New England Colonial home, noting how much time he had before the diner opened. He always wanted to live in a log cabin, but his wife couldn't bring herself to sell the home she was raised in after her parents passed on, so he renovated it to their liking.

She got the large kitchen with the fancy appliances and an eight-foot wood dining table and chairs for Thanksgiving dinners so she could invite all their friends. His room was the family room, the one she mockingly referred to as his man cave.

There was an enormous back deck off the kitchen with a gorgeous view of the mountains. He remodeled it into a four-season room with a cathedral ceiling, wood beams, windows on three sides—

leaving the view—and he built a stone fireplace with a spot for the flat-screen TV above it. He cut down the walnut tree in the backyard and used the wood to build cabinets on both sides and finished them with glass doors. The grandfather clock stood in one corner of the room and a ten-foot, handcrafted wood pole stood in another, where the American Flag was proudly displayed.

Photographs and memories from his time in the military, antique weapons he brought back with him, or collected through the years, and medals and flags invaluable to him were all locked inside the glass cabinet doors. He also stored some of his regular weapons on the shelves, such as the Glocks he no longer used, and the various knives he carried during his time in service. A Sig Sauer P226 was in another glass case over the fireplace. His personal weapons, his wife's jewelry, bonds, and thousands in cash from his time as a private contractor were kept in a safe in the bedroom closet upstairs.

He glanced toward a photograph of him with his two buddies: Slim and Donnie, the three amigos, everybody called them. They were inseparable back then. Life, jobs, and family got in the way years later. He did that a lot lately, reminiscing. He and Donnie remained tight, and wound up living just a few miles away from each other after they left the service and private contracting work. Donnie became a cop. Mackie built a small construction company. And Slim went into politics, first becoming a member of Congress, and now he was a United States Senator, which gave him little time for his old pals. When Donnie was killed, Slim and Mackie reunited at the funeral, but the time and distance changed things.

Mackie had to come to terms with the fact that the three amigos were not the young pups they once were.

He smiled to himself. "But I've still got my memories."

He used the remote starter to start his black Chevy Silverado truck parked in the driveway. While it warmed up, he grabbed the bottle of homemade solution from under the kitchen sink and meticulously wiped down the glass on his cabinets, removing all the particles of dust from the day before. He verified they were still locked, put the cloth and solution back in their place, and headed outside. Something caused him to hesitate before stepping up into the truck; he felt like he was being watched. Years of being in the military and serving as a private contractor, he was always on alert, even all these years later.

The closest house was to the south, a half-mile down the road and on the same side of the street. A new fifty-five and over subdivision had been developed a mile up the hill to his north, and most of them were already occupied.

He studied the wooded landscape across the street, from left to right. His hearing was no help; too many gunshot blasts near his eardrums over the years made him deaf in one ear. When his wife used to tease him about not paying attention, his favorite line was: honey, I'm deaf in one ear and can't hear out the other. All he could see were trees with barely any leaves left and the crows that flocked to the area every morning were flying overhead. He noticed nothing out of the ordinary, but he couldn't shake the feeling either. After nearly a minute, he chalked it up to his imagination, stepped up into the driver's seat and reversed out of the driveway.

He headed south. At the four-way intersection at the end of the street, he turned right and headed into town. He continued onto the bridge with the fast-flowing Chestnut Falls River underneath. As beautiful as the river was, it could also be dangerous, especially during certain times of the year. At 1A, he turned left and made the first right turn into the parking lot for the diner. He pulled into his usual spot, backed in, and locked it after he stepped out. Never used to have to do that, he mused to himself.

"Good morning," he said to each local he passed, as he did every morning, and nodded to the young hostess behind the counter when he walked inside and took his usual seat.

"Morning, Mackie," she said with a smile as he bypassed her and the sign that said: wait to be seated. He was as well-known at the diner as the scent of the vanilla and cinnamon from the homemade French toast that greeted everyone each morning at the door.

"How's your morning going so far, Mackie?" she asked when she dropped off the menu, though she knew that was a waste of time. He ordered the same meal every day.

He glanced at her with a smile and a gleam in his eyes. "Every day I get up is a good day," he said, putting the menu off to the side like he did every morning.

"Well, you're looking chipper. How's that cough?"

He shrugged. "Barely notice it anymore," he said, but now that she had him thinking about it, he hoped it was nothing. He didn't want to interrupt his week

11

having to take a drive to the doctor's office, only to be told he just needed some chicken soup.

"Well, take care. Your waitress will be with you shortly."

~~~

Minutes after the black truck disappeared from sight, a white van with black lettering showing it was from the local power company, parked a few hundred yards north of the home.

There were two men inside. Stefan was in the driver's seat, Cole riding shotgun. Both wore black fatigues, gloves, and balaclavas with microphones clipped to their shirts. Cole continued to scope out the area with his military-grade binoculars to verify that Mackie didn't return.

"Subject exited the home," he said into the microphone, even though Stefan was sitting in the seat right next to him.

"Okay, we have our orders," Stefan said. "Remember, this is a smash and grab. We cut the power to avoid cameras, and then get what we came for, but make it look like a robbery in case the cops are called."

Cole gave Stefan a sideways glance. "You told me we wouldn't have to worry about the cops."

"And I stand by my original assessment," Stefan said, annoyed that he had to repeat himself. "It is highly unlikely the homeowner will involve law enforcement considering the trouble that could ensue if what we're after became public."

"What the hell? If the guy's worried about the shit going public, why do we have to steal it to keep it from happening?"

Stefan shrugged. "You just answered your own question, in part. But besides making sure it never sees the light of day, the client will have some leverage if he has the information in his possession. That's over our pay-grade so we don't question it."

Cole did one more check of the area. Mackie's house was the only one on this stretch of the road, but someone could walk a dog or jog through the area from the subdivision up the street. Once they deemed it all clear, they filed out.

From their surveillance over the last two weeks, they learned there were security cameras on the front and back doors, and one over the garage, but they couldn't verify the location of any cameras inside. They weren't concerned about Mackie seeing them in their masks, but they wanted to avoid him studying their movements inside the home. They were after something specific, and it was in their best interest not to let on.

Stefan ducked down to the left side of the driveway to avoid the camera over the door, just in case Mackie set it to alert him on the phone. When he reached the garage, he ducked under the camera above and cut over into the backyard. Staying low to avoid the other camera in the back, he sidled up against the clapboard siding until he reached the electric panel box. He opened it and flipped the switch to cut off the power.

"Okay to enter," he said into the microphone. When he returned to join his partner in front of the house, Cole had already used the lock picking gun and unlocked the door. They slipped inside, closed the door behind them, and stood in the entryway while they regrouped.

"What did you pick up from your surveillance of the interior over the last two weeks?" Cole asked.

"The guy is a stickler for routines."

"I know what we're after, just not the location," Cole said.

"We're looking for bookshelves he designed from a walnut tree that he cut down and enclosed with glass cabinets."

Cole studied the layout of the interior. "Then probably a living room or family room,"

They worked their way through the house, started in the living room at the front of the house to the right of the entry. The room was meticulously neat, the floor pristine, and the potted plants were as green as if they were in the tropics. There was not a speck of dust in the room. An antique Victorian style sofa, upholstered in off-white fabric, was positioned in the center of the room facing a large front window that offered a view of the wooded landscape across the street. A sofa table sat behind it with two floral plants at each end, and two wingback chairs were positioned on each side of the coffee table in its front. There was also a grand piano in the far corner that also looked untouched, as if someone dusted and waxed it daily. The service gleamed, making it appear as though it was wrapped in a sheet of acrylic.

Stefan ran a gloved finger across the sofa table, noting the glossy sheen on his fingertip from a layer of protection. "Doesn't look like he used this room, other than his disciplined cleanings."

"Good thing," Cole said, looking out at the view from the sofa. "He could have spotted us during our surveillance over the last two weeks. He was military. He'd know what to look for."

14

Stefan dismissed the comment with a wave of his hand. "He's been off the FOB, field of battle, for some time."

The men continued into the kitchen. They knew from their research on Mackie that his wife had been dead a few years, but it still smelled like the cinnamon of an apple pie being baked in the oven. They finally entered the family room and admired the mountain views through the windows. Then they focused their attention on the stone fireplace with wood and glass cabinets on both sides.

Stefan marched toward the cabinet to the left and studied the old military photographs, showing Mackie and his two buddies, one of which is now a senator. Some photos showed them in their uniforms. In others, they were in plain clothes on liberty. A local woman was photographed with them in three different images.

"So these guys got friendly with a local in Damascus who was involved with our client back when they were private contractors?" Cole asked. "What's the big deal? That was two decades ago."

Stefan shook his head and smirked. "The client is running for a higher office. The woman disappeared while they were in Syria. Gossip, conspiracy theories, and speculation that she was murdered followed. He doesn't want images of her to surface during his campaign, causing questions for the press. He has his reasons, and we don't need to know what they are."

"No shit," Cole said. "Is this like a Kennedy situation?"

Stefan shrugged. "Less we know, the better off we are."

"Would just be nice to know why, that's all," Cole said, genuinely curious.

Stefan stopped what he was doing and glared at his partner. "Did you not pick up on the fact that the woman disappeared and could be dead? Or maybe she's not and living a good life, but he doesn't want the press to connect the two of them. Bottom line: we don't need to know. When we're hired to fix a problem, we don't ask questions that could also get us in trouble."

"Yeah, I get it," Cole said after a minute.

Stefan retrieved his flashlight from a loop on his belt, stood off to the side, and slammed the flashlight into the glass, shattering it into slivers and shards of glass on the ground.

"Why didn't we just pick the lock?"

"This sends a better message," Stefan said. "To a cop, it will look like a robbery. Mackie will assume what we were after and keep his mouth shut."

Cole shrugged and then repeated the move on the glass in front of him. He opened the large duffel bag, snatched the antique weapons, and placed them inside. He did the same with the handheld guns.

Stefan loaded all the framed photographs into the corner of the duffel, and then snatched the war medals and flags that were also stored inside.

Cole pulled out one medal and studied it. "The Silver Star? Was this guy a war hero?"

"Does it matter?"

"Guess not. Orders are orders."

"Alright then, don't worry about it."

Once they had taken everything from the cabinets, Stefan noticed a Sig Sauer in a smaller glass case on the mantel over the fireplace. He walked toward it, smashed the glass case, and pulled the gun free.

"What about the second floor?" Cole asked, motioning toward the stairs opposite the living room.

Stefan checked the magazine on the gun. "We've got enough. Set up the recording device as instructed; it's time to go."

Cole looked around the room. He walked toward the coffee table in front of the sofa. His boots crunched over the glass, tracking slivers into the pristine wood floor as he moved. He picked up the black ink pen that was positioned next to magazines and replaced it with a voice-activated writing pen from his shirt pocket. He could make any adjustments to the app he had on his cell once he was back inside the van. The pen was very similar in appearance to the one Mackie had, and would write just the same, so he wasn't worried about it being detected, but it could also record conversations. He placed a second one in the kitchen, next to Rosie's notepads.

Cole opened the front door wide enough to look outside. Not seeing anyone, they stepped out into the brisk weather, shut the door behind them, and marched back toward the van. Once they were several hundred feet away, Stefan took off the balaclava. The sweat irritated him and made the balaclava itch the whiskers on his face. He strode toward the back of the van to put the duffel bag inside. That's where he came face-to-face with an older gentleman who had been walking his schnauzer dog and was currently looking inside the back window.

The man's eyes went wide and his mouth dropped open, seeing Stefan dressed in black, wearing gloves, and armed with a gun.

His dog growled.

"You're not with the power company. Who the hell are you guys, and what were you doing in Mackie's house?"

Stefan had a split second to make a decision. Their orders were to leave no evidence that could trace back to them or the client who hired them. No evidence also meant no witnesses.

And this guy saw his face.

"You're not supposed to be here," the man continued, reaching for his cell phone. "I'm calling the sheriff."

It wouldn't be the first time he killed. After an incident in Iraq, he and his partner were both discharged from the military. He was lucky they weren't sent to the brig. He realized then that he should have left the damn balaclava on.

He raised the Sig Sauer. The older man's eyes bulged out of the sockets. He turned around to run the other way, but because of his age, he wasn't fast enough. A bullet penetrated him through the side of the head and the man fell to the ground.

Hearing the commotion, followed by the gunshot, Cole rushed to the back of the van. "What the hell, man? Why'd you shoot him?"

Stefan glared at him. "He saw my face. The man said no evidence."

"Damn," Cole said, as he started pacing. "No evidence doesn't have to equal murder. Shit, man, I thought we left all that behind when we were discharged."

"Don't be naïve, man," Stefan shouted. "What we collected could be used as political opposition against a candidate for a future president. It's not called dirty politics for nothing. You accepted that when you came on board. This is the big leagues, not a campaign for high school class president."

"Well, what the hell do we do now?"

Stefan looked around. There was still nobody around, only the barking dog. "Hide him in the woods," he said. "We'll dump the gun on the way out of town. If they find it, they won't trace it back to us, anyway."

Cole took a deep breath and thought it through. He needed this gig, and it paid good money. After his discharge from the army, he'd been floundering from one lame job to another. He was so desperate he sold meth for a while until the dealer was busted, with him safely out of the crosshairs. This job could work out for him, financially, with a big bonus if they did what they were told. Then he could buy himself a small place up in the mountains somewhere and live a comfortable life. Besides, he wasn't the one who took off his mask or took a shot at the guy. If it came back on Stefan, he was still in the clear. Either way, they better wrap it up. Mackie could be back soon.

While Stefan loaded the duffle into the back of the van, Cole fireman-carried the man into the woods across the street from Mackie's house and hid him among a pile of branches and leaves. The dog followed him, and grabbed a hold of his ankle and bit hard, causing him to yelp out in pain. He tried to shoo the dog away, which only increased the barking.

"Damn dog, just bit me," Cole said into the microphone.

"Well, shut the damn thing up," Stefan said, shaking his head at Cole's feeble attempts to chase the dog down, but not having any luck.

"I'm not shooting a dog," Cole said.

Looking at his watch and realizing time was short, Stefan marched into the woods. "Then just grab the frigging leash. You can't leave the dog here. It could just alert somebody to its owner's dead body before we're out of the area."

Cole finally grabbed the end of the leash, pulled the dog toward the van, and put him in the back. He would not let Stefan harm a defenseless dog. It was bad enough that he shot its owner. He was the one amateurish enough to remove his mask.

Another quick sweep of the area, the two men jumped into the driver and passenger seat of the van. Stefan cranked over the engine and sped off down the road. When they reached the town center of Whispering Oak, they pulled into the back alley behind the local hardware store, dropped the fired weapon into the dumpster, and left the van's door open so the dog could jump out.

Once they were back on the road, Cole looked into the rear-view mirror: the schnauzer was standing by the dumpster, barking. He frowned. He hoped it wouldn't be too long before somebody came along. It didn't feel right leaving the dog alone, especially not near the location where Stefan dropped the gun. Oh well, at least his fingerprints weren't on the weapon. Once they drove to another isolated town and torched the van with their clothing and gear inside, there was nothing else to get rid of. Another look through his mirror, he spotted Mackie's black truck parked on the side of the road by the Chestnut Falls River. He was just sitting there, looking out at the flowing river and the waterfall at the river's end. Was he mourning his lost wife, or reminiscing about his former life? Cole had a moment of doubt, especially since he saw the guy earned medals during his time in the war. All he achieved during his stint in Iraq was to listen to Stefan and make poor decisions, which forced them out. He knew to keep those thoughts to himself. Stefan would just remind him that politics is dirty business, and he willingly signed on for the check. Didn't mean he had to feel good about it.

CHAPTER 1 - KATIE

IT'S BEEN SEVERAL months since my cottage was burned down, which means I'm still living in the RV that Derek Jameson—the father of the stalker responsible for making me homeless—parked in the driveway for me to use. It's not as bad as one might think. The space is smaller, but I still have all the comforts of home. The leather sofas and reclining captain chairs are comfortable, the fireplace gives off enough heat and ambiance, and the large flat-screen smart TV is perfect for streaming films and TV series. It's also great because I can keep up on the renovations of the cottage through the windows that run up and down the length of the RV.

There are also a few downsides, but nothing earth-shattering: an RV washing machine can only handle small loads—which means a trip to the laundry mat for the bedding. The shower is a fraction of the size of the one in the cottage, so I can't move around as much. And the RV windows get steamed up when cooking, which causes the small space to heat-up like a sauna.

I put the ingredients together for two homemade quiches and had them backing in the oven for a late breakfast. I haven't been all that domesticated since my recent divorce, and the fact that I *am living in an RV*, but I was in the mood for a home-cooked meal.

I hurried to open the windows behind the leather sofas, opened the ceiling vent in the kitchen, and switched on the fan. Bailey looked up at me from her spot by the stove.

"I know, Bailey, it's hot," I said.

Finn was on his way over after finishing up at the gun club. He was placed on leave from the department after getting shot in the abdomen in the parking lot behind the police station after my last case. Thankfully, the bullet was a through and through, so the wound didn't impact any vital organs. I returned the favor and helped to nurse him back to health, as he did for me when I was shot in the shoulder. His recovery was a lot quicker. He was back to doing light desk duty at the police department until he completed his psych evaluation and re-qualified with his gun. Standard procedure after getting shot.

"Oh crap, he's here," I said, seeing the Dodge Charger when it pulled into the driveway. Bailey and I passed each other as I dashed back over to the oven, and she raced to the door with her tail whipping back and forth to welcome her friend.

I grabbed the oven mitts and slipped them on, then pulled both trays out and placed them on the wood cutting board. I turned the oven off, just as Finn tapped three times on the door.

Bailey barked in excitement. When he opened the door, she barked again. It was her way of saying hello.

"Hey girl," he said, putting his face down to her level and letting her lick him on the cheek. You wouldn't know she was my dog when Finn came around.

"How did it go?" I asked from my spot by the stove.

He shut the RV door behind him and strode toward me in his cavalier mode. The smile on his face was my answer, but I knew he'd provide me with more.

"Like riding a bicycle," he teased, pulling me in for a hug and kiss. "Something smells good, and not just the food."

"I thought you might be hungry after spending the morning doing tedious labor," I said with a smile. According to Finn, there was nothing tedious about spending time at the gun range. As former military and now a cop, he lived and breathed guns. He even designed two obstacle training courses on a large piece of land he owned out in the hills. One is for physical agility, similar to that of a course one would go through in a police academy. He says it keeps him fresh with his fitness level out in the field. The other is a training course that helps him prepare for hostage-type situations. Even though I'm not a police officer, he takes me there occasionally and pushes me through the course as if I was.

Finn noticed the two pans on the cutting board, and his face lit up with a smile. "Are those homemade quiches?"

I smiled in return. "With you going back to work, I assumed our time for home-cooked meals would be hit or miss. So—"

He wrapped his arms around my waist. "That was the upside to both of us getting shot; all that time we had together trying to recuperate."

"Hmm, it was nice," I said, allowing the imagery to flash through my eyes, which brought a twinkle to his eyes as well.

"Well, getting lucky in a hospital shower wasn't how I saw our first time going down, but it worked," he teased.

Before Finn was shot, we planned to get away to a B and B to enjoy some alone time, which meant having sex for the first time without interruptions. Since that couldn't happen, the two of us were left feeling anxious. On his third day in the hospital, I was helping him into the shower and we both just lost control, like two love-struck teenagers. It wound up being quick with both of us laughing most of the time, concerned the nurse would walk in and catch us. What it did was free us from the worry about our first time; though the next time wasn't much better, as far as the pre-planning stages go. I was at his house, with his mom and son, both in the family room. I was supposed to be helping him with his bandages, well you get the drift. Again, it was quick, because we kept hearing noises that sounded like his mother was traipsing down the hall to check up on us. And trust me; she would do that. We laugh about it now, especially since we no longer feel the pressure.

He released me, studied the label on the orange juice bottle on the table, and walked toward the cabinet where I keep the glasses. "Want me to pour the juice?"

"I won't say no."

Bailey followed him. It was almost as if she knew he was going back to full-time cop work and wouldn't be around much, so she was staying close.

I reached into the refrigerator, grabbed the bowl of fruit, and placed it on the table. Then I picked up his plate, used the spatula, and loaded his plate with a slice of each. One was filled with spinach, onions, and tomatoes, the other sausage and peppers.

"So you passed the gun re-qualification, what about the psych evaluation report?"

He dismissed the subject with a wave of his hand. "She verbally signed off. Maldonado said that's good enough, for now. I'm more concerned with my stamina after taking the hit. I'll be spending the next few days at the gym, upping my sit-ups, push-ups, and running time, and working on some breathing techniques I used to do during my days in special ops."

With our glasses filled, he sat down. "Do you have any red pepper?"

I gave him a sideways glance. "You should try it first, before you add more. I already seasoned it to your liking with fresh garlic and pepper."

He took a taste but still added the red pepper. *The man likes his food hot.*

I made a plate for myself and sat down opposite him. We sat in silence for a couple of minutes while we devoured our food. Then my cell phone vibrated, interrupting the blissful quiet. Viewing the screen, I could see that it was a call from dad's best friend, Mackie, who served in the military with him.

"I have to take this," I told Finn.

He nodded, too distracted by the quiches to care.

"Hi, Uncle Mackie," I said. He wasn't really my uncle. It was just a habit I picked up as a child and continued into adulthood. As my dad's best friend, he was around a lot.

"Hey Kid," he said. "Hope I'm not interrupting anything."

"Of course not," I said. "It's good to hear from you. It's been a while."

"Sorry to say, this call is not for pleasure," he said.

"Are you okay?" My first thought was that he had some kind of health issue. He has always been physically fit, but at seventy, even the healthiest could run into a medical issue.

"No, nothing like that," he said. "Gonna take more than hitting senior status to knock me down."

If it wasn't a health issue, then what was it? I could tell by the tone of his voice that whatever was on his mind wasn't good. Like my dad always said; Mackie wore his feelings on his sleeve. He was an open book. I moved away from the table and sat down on the leather sofa so Finn could enjoy his meal, and I could concentrate on what he was saying.

"I need you to come to Whispering Oak."

I sat up straight. I promised my father I'd show up if Mackie ever called. Until now, he never did. Something was up. "Fill me in, Uncle Mackie."

"My home's been burglarized," he said. I could hear the distinctive anger in his voice by the change in his tone. "They took my medals, and your dad's."

I gasped. Mackie was the recipient of the Purple Heart during his time in Vietnam. Dad also earned a Purple Heart, but it was his Silver Star that the two of them held dear. Only those warriors that served on the front lines together would understand. To them, they were more valuable than money. My father gifted it to Mackie upon his death, along with a personal note that I wasn't privy to.

"I'll be there as soon as I can, Uncle Mackie."

CHAPTER 2 - KATIE

MY NAME IS Katie Parker. I am a private investigator with an office in Onset, Massachusetts, though I cover most of Cape Cod, or anywhere else the potential case leads me, which is presently the town of Whispering Oak. Along with the PI license, the state has also extended me the privilege of packing heat. In layman's terms, that means I get to walk around in public carrying a gun. Of course, they advised I keep the gun out of sight and practice using it from time to time, but that doesn't detract from the feeling of power I feel just knowing it's there. Finn, the hot undercover cop I've been seeing, suggested I try a Glock, but I haven't taken the plunge yet, instead opting to keep the .38 Smith & Wesson my father taught me to use, which I keep at my hip in my leather gun belt. During the winter months, my bomber jacket hides it, abiding by the rules to keep it out of sight.

I have not visited the small town of Whispering Oak since I buried my father. Mackie was a tremendous support to me then. The two men have always been tight, like brothers. They did a ten-year tour together in Vietnam and then finished out the next ten years at various bases. Still relatively young when they retired from the military, they served two years as private contractors so they could put away some cash, providing security for members of the CIA and politicians at the embassy in various foreign countries. Ironic that they made more cash in those two years than the twenty they served. My father's favorite quote: 'service to the country is not about financial reward' helped me to understand.

When they returned to civilian life, my dad became a police officer, and Mackie started a small construction business. They didn't do much talking about their time in the military in front of me. They saved those talks for when I wasn't around. I always wondered why, but didn't want to push.

There was a third member who joined their crew periodically: Hal Colson, known as Slim to them back then. He also served in Nam and met up with them again when they served as PMCs in Damascus. They were thick as thieves during their time in service, but Hal went on to bigger things after he left the military. He ran for a seat in congress and then became a senator for the State of Maine. The three men kept in touch through the years; my father and Mackie always included Hal when they planned a bonding weekend of hunting, fly-fishing, 18 rounds of golf, or a NASCAR race. Sometimes Hal showed up, other times, he had a family or work scheduling conflict. I didn't see as much of him as I did of Mackie, but he made it to my father's funeral, even though he was surrounded by security.

I knew there was a bond between the three men; one, because of the photographs my father kept of their time during the military, and also because he made me promise to always be available if either of them ever reached out. He told me Mackie was the reason he lived to be a father. When I asked him how, he told me it was Mackie's story to tell.

~~~

When my vehicle rolled up to the sign alerting me I was entering the town of Whispering Oak, a flood of memories flashed before my eyes, mostly good, even though my father was buried in the quaint town. He moved to the area a few years before I married my former husband, Jake. My father had little luck with finding a good wife. He met my mother in the military when they were first enlisted. Once I turned two, she wanted out. Living in a small town and raising a child by herself while he continued to serve was not her cup of tea. The woman he married when I was five-years old was worse, though I could see how she put on the charm when they first met. My father was always a sucker for a pretty face. He only learned of the ugliness inside later. Thankfully, he had Mackie's friendship to fall back on.

Mackie and his wife, Rosie, moved into her childhood home in Whispering Oak after her parents died. Dad helped them with the renovations. In between his shifts at the police department and working on the house, they spent hours on the golf course in the spring and summer, and took to the mountains for hunting in the winter. The hobby that took me by surprise was the fly-fishing the two men took up and enjoyed along the Chestnut Falls River. When I was growing up, my dad hated fishing. Said there was nothing more boring than sitting and watching a pole. Maybe fly-fishing offered more adventure. After a while, dad realized it made more sense to make Whispering Oak his new place of residence instead of spending hours driving back and forth. I often wondered if Rosie knew she was getting a package deal when she married Mackie.

I drove down Main Street, reminded of the wholesome beauty and welcoming feel of the town. It felt like driving into a modern version of Andy Griffith's Mayberry R.F.D. The first two blocks of the street housed the municipal buildings, most of them brick exterior expected in a New England town. Restaurants, antique shops, and chain convenient stores and full-service-pump gas stations were mixed in between. No self serve. While driving, I also noticed there were no fast-food spots, Dunkin Donuts or Starbucks in the area, which meant the residences, nearly five-thousand as of the last census report, wanted to keep the drive-thru establishments out of the area.

I continued until the street branched off and turned into 1A. Every time I visited my father in the area, I spent most of my time walking along that street. Both the Whispering Oak Diner and bookstore and café—converted from an old mill—were within a few blocks from each other and places I frequented. Being an author before my cottage was torched, and my computers and manuscripts inside of it, I was fortunate enough to have a few book signings at the bookstore. There were three floors, each one offering a view of the Chestnut Falls River and the mountains in the distance. A couple times, I went there just to relax, purchased a book and spent most of the day on the outside patio of the café reading while enjoying the view.

I crossed over the bridge that took me over the river and followed the car's GPS directions to Mackie's house. I had been there before, a few times in fact, but it had been a while. When I turned onto Mackie's street, I noticed police action in the woods across the street from his house. Two sheriff SUVs with blue and red lights flashing were parked in front of the woods. When I pulled into his driveway, shut off the engine, and stepped out, I noticed two deputies with windbreakers, gloves and booties on their feet combing through the wooded area. Another young man with crime scene tech on the back of his windbreaker finished wrapping yellow crime tape around trees to keep residents from walking through.

When Mackie called, he mentioned he didn't want the sheriff involved yet, so I was surprised they were in the area. They weren't technically on his property. They were in the wooded area across the street from his home, so what were the odds they were in the area on an unrelated matter? I wasn't one to believe in coincidences, but I wouldn't know until I spoke with Mackie. Focusing back on his house, I spotted him sitting in a rocking chair on his front porch, waving me forward.

"Uncle Mackie, what's going on?" I asked him, motioning toward the crime scene tape.

His expression was subdued. "Dead body. A neighbor from the subdivision a mile up the road. He's a little younger than me, but not by much. He usually walks his dog this way."

I studied him. "What drew you there?"

"The crows were making a lot of racket, more than usual," he said, raking his hand through his white hair. "I thought maybe there was a dead deer or other animal; wouldn't be the first time. I went to check it out. That's when I found him. I shooed the crows away, so they didn't disturb the scene. Then I stayed with the body while I called it in to wait for the Sheriff."

"What happened to him, heart attack?" I couldn't imagine what other ailment would cause a man to die while walking his dog.

He rubbed his hands down his face, obviously distressed over the death of somebody he knows. "Somebody shot him."

I gasped and my eyes went wide as I looked toward the wooded area. Again, I was reminded that I wasn't a believer of coincidences. Not that they couldn't happen, they just usually don't. And on the same day Mackie's home was burglarized?

"Sheriff already questioned me," he said. "The body was still warm, so they knew it happened sometime this morning. I was at the diner when it opened."

"So the death was possibly around the same time your home was burglarized?"

"Sheriff won't know the official time of death until she talks with the ME. But it sure as hell is not sitting right with me. I kept the burglary to myself for the time being."

I studied him, wondering why.

"Where's the man's dog?"

"Haven't found her yet.

I reached the top of the stairs and he pulled me into a hug. "Thank you for coming, Katie," he said.

"It's good to see you," I said, welcoming his embrace.

"You didn't bring Bailey?" he asked, looking for her. He loved throwing the ball with her and seeing her infectious energy, just like Finn and Derek's assistant, Loretta.

"No, she's staying with my boss, Derek, who also has two dogs. I wasn't sure how long I'd be here, or how involved the case would be."

Suddenly distracted, Mackie waved at someone passing by. When I followed his eyes, I noticed it was the sheriff leaving the scene. She rolled past in her SUV and waved, showing they were on friendly terms. Small towns, everybody knows each other, so why wouldn't he tell her about the break-in?

"Show me what happened, Uncle Mackie."

He opened his door and ushered me inside. "They came in through the front door," he said. "They must have picked the lock, but left it unlocked when they left the premises. I didn't need my key to get in."

We stood inside the doorway so I could check things out. I set my laptop bag down by the door and pulled a pair of latex gloves from the front flap and slipped them on. If we wound up calling in the sheriff, I didn't want any additional fingerprints, though I suspected the people who did this probably wore gloves as well. First, I studied the lock on his door. Whatever lock-picking tool they used, they definitely didn't leave behind any evidence that they did so.

I followed him into a beautiful living room. The room was so perfect it looked professionally staged, as if it was being showcased to sell to potential buyers. I could tell it had been meticulously cared for, even though his wife had passed some time ago. It was so clean Mackie could point out a mark on his sofa table.

"The homemade solution I used to wipe down the surface leaves a gloss," he said, as if he needed to explain. "Whoever did this purposely ran their gloved fingerprint across the top."

That's odd, I thought to myself, but I registered it in my mind for later.

We continued through Rosie's fabulous kitchen that was left untouched, and then stood in the doorway to the family room, where I could see all the smashed glass. The room was a man's delight. The floor was wide-pine wood planks. A deep brown leather sofa faced the fireplace and the seventy-inch flat-screen TV above it, with antique wood end tables at both ends. Two matching recliners sat on each side, yet they were angled so whoever sat in them could see the TV. An afghan that I assumed was crocheted by Rosie was draped across a square wood coffee table that Mackie built. Hunting, weapons, and fly-fishing books sat on top, with a black writing pen next to them.

I knew from early conversations with my father that Mackie renovated the house to his and Rosie's specifications and built most of the wood furniture inside the home. I haven't been upstairs, but my father told me about the four-poster bed Mackie made from the same walnut tree that he used to build his cabinets.

"And you said on the phone that they didn't go upstairs?"

He shook his head. "Nope."

I shook my head. "Not a typical robbery."

I could see from Mackie's expression that he felt the same, though he didn't elaborate just yet. He was rather subdued, which was understandable after finding a dead body.

All the other rooms were left untouched, except for the purposeful gloved fingerprint on the sofa table. It was only what was behind the glass cabinets and his gun on the fireplace that had been stolen. After he phoned me about the robbery, he texted me a list of items that were taken. Everything was from his and my father's time in the military and the two years they served as private contractors. Some items on the list were gifts from my father. It was the photographs that struck me as odd. Why would somebody steal photographs of my father, Mackie, and their third friend, Hal Colson, when the three of them served together? It was so long ago.

"Mackie, do you have a reason for not wanting to get the sheriff involved right now, especially considering the dead body?" I asked, genuinely curious.

"I do, but I can't say just set. I need to talk with someone before I do." The look on his face made me wonder if he had mistrust for law enforcement in this area, but I quickly dismissed that. It was a small town with one sheriff and only a few deputies. When she drove by, Mackie waved and smiled. He wouldn't have done so if he had an issue with them.

"You said it yourself. This wasn't a typical robbery. I've got thousands of dollars' worth in electronics and other items spread throughout the house, and even more in cash inside the safe upstairs, which they could have stolen and figured out how to get it open off site."

I nodded. "What about your security cameras?"

"They shut off the electricity," he said through clenched teeth, "but one of my cameras caught something before they cut the power. Unfortunately, I was enjoying my coffee and omelet and didn't pay attention to a motion alert notification from the app on my phone when I was at the diner."

He pulled out his cell phone, opened the app for his cameras, and scrolled through several short video clips until he found the one he was looking for and hit play: It appeared to be a shot from a camera above his garage that showed footage of his driveway. As the video played, it showed Mackie step up into his black truck and reverse out of the driveway, and the time he did so.

"That was me leaving for the diner," he said, exciting out of the clip and opening another.

Seconds passed and then something shot across the screen where the driveway met the street. It went by so fast I wasn't sure what I had just seen. It was too tall to be a deer, or other animal, unless it was a bear, but that was doubtful, and the image was blurry. Maybe it was someone jogging by the house.

"Can you slow that down?"

He stopped the video, hit rewind, and slowed the timing of the sequence. This time, when he hit play, the blurry image moved in slow motion. And now, I could tell it was a person. From the size, I assumed male, and he was dressed in black from head to toe, which meant he was wearing a mask.

"Slow it a little more," I said. "This time, when you're viewing it, tell me it doesn't look like a man wearing tactical gear with tools in the cargo pockets on the sides."

Mackie stared at me, but did as I suggested and agreed he saw the same thing. "So you agree it's probably a professional."

So you agree; meaning he thought that before he called me.

"Well, it's definitely not some fly-by-night burglar," I said. I held his phone and stopped the image so that we had a full-view.

"Definitely not a novice," he said, but I could tell he was still holding something back.

"This is a small town without stores that sell clothing or military gear. Odds are low that some novice came equipped and only chose one room in the house to steal from. The guy knew how to bypass the cameras and shut off the power without being seen. If he was just a wannabe burglar, why would he pick your house? There are plenty of wealthy folks in this town, and why only the glass cabinets?"

He looked away, almost as if he was avoiding me. "They were after something."

"And my gut tells me somebody has been scoping out the area and they were watching you."

Mackie frowned. "I got a sense that I was being watched this morning when I was leaving my driveway, but I dismissed it."

I studied the locks on the walnut cabinet door. "It also seemed rather personal. If they were professionals, they could have picked the lock to get into those cabinets. Instead, they maliciously shattered the glass. Mackie, was there something significant inside those cabinets that was valuable enough to someone, other than you and my father, that they didn't want you to have them?"

The look on his face made me frown, because he wasn't ready to confide in me just yet.

"Well, I can't force you, but I think you should notify the sheriff. It could get worse, if you don't."

"I need to get in touch with somebody first, and then we'll do this together."

I took photographs, especially the cabinets and shattered glass, and then we taped off the room. Even if he told the sheriff, he still wanted me to investigate on my own. That was telling, but as my father's long-time friend, I knew he had his reasons.

He texted me a copy of the camera footage of the blurred figure, provided me with the names of individuals depicted in the photographs stolen from his cabinet, and serial numbers of the weapons that were taken so I could contact local pawn shops. Neither of us thought this was about money, but I needed to be thorough.

Before I started anything, I would need to get a place to stay for a few nights, so I at least had a local base to work out of. Mackie wanted me to stay with him, but I suggested we wait until we learned what this was all about. Once he informed the sheriff of the break-in, deputies would need to photograph and attempt to collect prints inside his home. I would just get in the way.

The next hour was spent walking around the exterior looking for any other signs of intruders. Mackie walked me around the backyard, showed me where his cameras were located, and the location of the electric panel where they shut off the power. There were no neighbors on either side or in the front and back. The nearest house was a half mile away. Mackie told me they were elderly and didn't get around much. Doubtful they would have noticed anything. Back on the front porch, I studied the wooded area across the street and the deputies combing the scene. It was my opinion that whoever did this had skills, whether former military or law enforcement.

"The man who was killed. Do you know where he lived?" I asked Mackie.

He pointed toward the road at the right of his house. "There's a development about a mile up the road for 55 and over. He walks his dog down this way. Sometimes, he would stop for a cup of coffee and a chat, especially after Rosie died. He lost his wife some years ago, so it was just him and his dog."

"Uncle Mackie, we really should talk to the sheriff," I said. I bet that the man whose body was found saw something, and he lost his life for it. "So whoever it is you need to call, you should probably do it now."

He hesitated and then nodded before walking toward the opposite end of the farmer's porch to make the call in private.

Leaving me with my own thoughts, I realized that the best way to find out who the perpetrators were might be to discover what they were after, and why.

CHAPTER 3 – THE FIXERS

STEFAN MICHAELS, A man of average looks—whose only noticeable trait was having a voice that sounded like, Alan Rickman, from *Die Hard*—sat at the foldout table inside a Ram Promaster conversion mobile camper as if he was the senior executive of a prestigious firm. That couldn't be further from the truth. In fact, many of his own friends have described him as a weasel of a man with no moral fiber, to which he would always smile and chuckle as if that was a badge of honor. After being dishonorably discharged from the army, he created Michaels Consulting Services (MCS) but he was mostly known as a fixer who did opposition research for politicians, and would push the boundaries with dirty, and sometimes malicious, tricks. He proved that from the disreputable backgrounds of those he worked with. One of which was his current client who would do anything necessary to achieve his goal, and his partner who was discharged along with him after an incident in Iraq. Stefan had an expensive laptop in front of him and his fingers punched away on the keyboard, as if he already overdosed on caffeine, or something stronger.

Behind him was a corkboard filled with images of former clients. Newspaper clippings of stories and propaganda narratives he pushed to self-serving journalists with their own agendas. Media stories about his current client photographed at various pressers which were being used to push a public relations campaign for a possible presidential run.

The headline on one of the former clippings was highlighted in yellow: THREE YEARS SINCE THE BODY OF POLITICAL STAFFER JEFF MYERS WAS DISCOVERED IN A WASHINGTON DC PARK; MURDERED AND STILL NO LEADS.

His present client, Thomas Edwin Xavier, was on the screen doing a face-time call on the computer, hoping for an update. He was a multi-millionaire and the founder of a firm that provided private security contractors, and he was currently conducting an exploratory committee for a potential presidential run. Although he served four years in the military, and then became a private military contractor, he was considered an outsider with no former political experience. He hired Stefan to do the dirty work and make sure there would be no skeletons uncovered once a campaign run was announced to the press, so that Xavier's security firm could be kept free from the independent journalists doing their own opposition research.

The Promaster camper was fully equipped to take on the road when a job called for daily travel. It offered a full-sized kitchen with appliances, a bathroom and shower, two separate sleeping quarters—one of which folded out to a table for working during the day—and it was customized with computers, electronics and satellite and Wi-Fi capability.

One of the leather captains' chairs was occupied by his partner Cole—they were the two men who had been keeping a tail on Mackie and burglarized the home. The photographs they took from the cabinets were scattered on top of the table and the other items were still in the duffel at the side of the table.

On a shelf to the right of Stefan, electronic equipment buzzed, and a dispatcher's voice echoed from a law enforcement scanner alerting them of calls in the town of Whispering Oak. Stefan rolled his eyes. So far, the only complaint they heard was when the dispatcher put out a call to a deputy to check the sump pump for an elderly woman whose basement was flooding, even though there had been no rain. There was also a call for a dead body, but the words used by the dispatcher made it appear as though it was a death by natural causes, probably done on purpose to keep nosey residents from crowding the scene and spreading fear.

"I told you he wouldn't alert the sheriff that he had been robbed," Stefan said, gloating. "Not with the secret he's keeping. It's a Podunk town; it'll probably be weeks before they find the gun."

Mr. Xavier gave him a stern look. "You still should have handled it better."

Stefan rolled his eyes, dismissing his client's words. "Xavier, it's easy for you to sit there in your comfy office telling us how things should get done, when it's the two of us out in the field getting our hands dirty."

"I told you to refer to me as Mr. Xavier or sir. We're not buddies here. I'm paying you good money. I expect some damn respect."

"Sorry, sir," Stefan said, begrudgingly. If it wasn't for the good money he was being paid, he would have told this client to screw.

"I told you this could blow back on us," Cole said, in a voice that was almost a whisper.

Stefan shrugged. "It was Mackie's gun. How could it blow back on us?"

44

"Smooth move," Mr. Xavier said sarcastically.

Stefan shrugged. "You told us no evidence or witnesses that could prove we were in the area. I specifically asked you what that meant. You said, and I quote: 'dead bodies are inevitable '."

Mr. Xavier cocked his head to the side. "I don't care about the dead body; it's not your first and won't be your last. I was referring to tossing the gun where you left the barking dog. As you said, it's a Podunk town. Neighbors are nosey in small towns. A barking dog is bound to draw attention. Did you think to remove the dog tag that will trace back to the owner, who has already been discovered?"

"What the fuck difference does it make?" Stefan argued. "You think a barking dog will alert a small-town sheriff or deputy to look in a dumpster? And even if they did, it will still trace back to the guy who owned the gun. We wore gloves. There's no trace of us left behind, other than the recording device you had Cole plant in the house."

On the laptop screen, Cole could see Mr. Xavier look in his direction. "Which reminds me; have you heard anything yet?"

Cole nodded. "He called in a private investigator."

"A private investigator?" Mr. Xavier glared at Cole. "To do what, exactly?"

Stefan smirked. "To investigate, I would imagine."

Mr. Xavier glared at Stefan. "Do I need to remind you who is paying the bills? I'm not paying for flip responses. Besides, wouldn't an investigator reveal that secret he wants to keep?"

"Investigators are paid to keep secrets," Stefan said, mocking his client. "Isn't that why you hired us?"

Mr. Xavier gave him a sardonic smile. "You should remember. I can fire you any time."

Stefan's face was a mask of stone.

Mr. Xavier dismissed him and turned his attention to Cole again. "What did he say when the investigator showed up? Do they have a clue what you were after?"

Cole shook his head. "They don't know what we were after, but she suspected it wasn't just a robbery, that we were there for something specific."

"She?" Mr. Xavier said, appearing to relax for a minute, as if the idea of a female investigator wasn't as intimidating.

Cole nodded. "Yeah, *she* thought it seemed personal."

Mr. Xavier sat up straight and frowned. "Why would she come to that conclusion?"

Cole glanced over at Stefan, and he looked hesitant to say.

"Don't hide behind your partner. What made her think this robbery was personal?"

Cole rubbed his hand across the back of his neck, sweat forming on his upper lip, nervous to be ratting out Stefan. "She said if it was a robbery by professionals, as she assumed we were, that we would have picked the locks to the cabinets—like we did at the front door—instead of smashing the glass all over the floor."

Mr. Xavier's eyes turned menacing. He leaned closer to his computer and glared at Stefan. "You couldn't do what I said, could you? You had to go off half-cocked and handle it your way. Of course, she thinks it's personal. She's right, but you weren't supposed to let on. You pointed them in the direction we were trying to avoid. I said make it look like a financial robbery."

"Don't be so dramatic," Stefan said, rolling his eyes again. "Just because they think it could be personal doesn't mean they'll figure out what the target was. They probably assume it was somebody after his restored weapons."

Cole nodded. "Stefan is probably right. I'm looking into the PI. Sounds like she was a friend."

Mr. Xavier breathed a sigh of relief and leaned back in his leather chair. "Right. No reason to be concerned yet. Do that; get a thorough background on the PI and keep tabs on her."

Stefan leaned forward with raised eyebrows. "And if she becomes someone to be concerned about? How far are you prepared to go to keep the secrets in the past?"

Mr. Xavier returned his glare. "I'm running an exploratory committee for the highest office. As far as it takes, just—"

"—I heard you before. Nothing we do will trace back to us, or you, because I'm good at what I do. Did they discover who supplied the fake images of your opposition that wound up on the cover of the tabloids the day he made his announcement? Did the media find out why several women who worked for your firm recanted the sexual assault allegations they made against you a decade ago?"

Mr. Xavier cocked his head to the side. "You threatened to show their current husbands and employers the images. That was malicious, not exactly clever."

Stefan shrugged. "They recanted, didn't they, and they've been keeping their mouths shut with a little reminder in the mail once it was leaked to the DC Post that you're exploring a run for President?"

A gleam appeared in Mr. Xavier's eyes. "Maybe we are on the same page, after all."

Stefan eyed his client. "It was you? You were the one who leaked the story to the post about the exploratory committee, weren't you?"

Mr. Xavier grabbed a cigar from a box and smiled. "It's all a game, Stefan. We're just starting it early. Keep me informed about the private investigator. And let me be clear; I don't care if you get your hands dirty, as long as you keep my name out of it."

When Stefan smiled, Cole looked a little uneasy.

CHAPTER 4 – KATIE

"MACKIE!" Gertrude said in a jovial manner from her seat behind the dispatch desk, like they were old friends. She got up, a huge smile plastered across her face as she rushed around and pulled him into a hug, even though he was a bear of a man and much larger than her. "What brings you here?"

"Afternoon Gertrude, this is Donnie's daughter, Katie," he said, using the nickname he called my father before he died. "She's in town to help me with a minor matter."

Gertrude shook Katie's hand in a warm welcome, her eyes wide in acknowledgment. "It's so good to meet you, Katie. We all miss your father. He was such a good man, not to mention easy on the eyes."

I shook her hand, and she clasped her other hand over mine. "Thank you, Gertrude. That's very nice of you to say."

"We're here to see the sheriff, Gertrude," Mackie said as she sat back down. "Is she available?"

"She's got a lot on her plate right now," Gertrude said, and then leaned in conspiratorially. "You heard about the dead body... oh wait, you called it in. Of course you did. Then, you understand."

"We have some information that might pertain to the situation she is currently dealing with," Katie interrupted.

"You don't say?" Gertrude looked back and forth at both of us, noticing the serious expression on our faces.

"She'll want to talk to us," Mackie added.

49

Gertrude nodded, picked up the phone, and dialed through to her office. "Sheriff Chase, you've got two visitors out front. It's Mackie and his friend, Katie. They claim to have more information regarding the dead body."

"Send them back," Sheriff Chase said.

Gertrude hung up the phone and pushed a button under her desk. "You can go on back. She's the last door on the right at the end of the hall."

At the sound of a buzzing noise, Mackie opened the door, allowed me to walk through and then followed me down the hall.

Sheriff Chase stood outside the door to her office, looking curious. "Afternoon Mackie, Gertrude tells me you have more info pertinent to my case?"

Mackie nodded. "Sheriff, this is Katie Parker. She is a private investigator, and a friend."

Sheriff Chase nodded and accepted the hand that I offered with a firm shake. "Good to meet you, Katie. Come on into my office, where we can talk."

She returned to her seat and motioned us toward the chairs opposite her desk.

"Sheriff, I wasn't completely forthcoming this morning when I spoke to you," Mackie said.

Her eyes narrowed, and a slight frown replaced her smile. "Oh? So you're here to rectify that?"

"I am." He looked down at his hands to avoid her probing eyes. He had never lied or withheld anything from her before.

She leaned back in her leather seat, glanced toward Katie for a moment, curious why a private investigator was with him.

"My home was burglarized this morning when I was at the diner. I know you don't have the exact time of death yet, but I assume the neighbor was shot before, during, or after the theft."

She leaned forward and placed her elbows down on the desk, and stared at Mackie. "What was taken?"

"They only seemed to be interested in the items I stored in my family room cabinets. My man cave, as Rosie used to call it. I had some restored weapons, and others I collected through the years, medals from the war, flags, etc."

Watching Mackie, I noticed he didn't mention the photographs which, for me, pointed toward their significance, so I made a mental note for later.

"They didn't go upstairs," he continued, "which would have been a nice reward for somebody looking for a financial windfall."

Sheriff Chase studied his mannerisms, but she held no suspicion in her eyes. I got the impression the two had a history of some sorts, even though he was reluctant to bring the case to her. Maybe he didn't want an official record?

"Is there a reason you failed to report this?"

He took a moment before answering, possibly to weigh his words carefully. "I wasn't aware of what happened to the neighbor when I first walked into my home and discovered the theft, and had already called Katie to help. After I discovered the body and called your deputies, I didn't want to believe the theft in my home got a man killed. I also didn't want the media to show up in my driveway, which I knew would happen if called it in to dispatch. That's why I came in to see you instead."

She took a moment to digest his response. "We're a small town, Mackie. I doubt the local newspaper has any qualified journalists hungry enough to camp out on your doorstep."

His shoulders lifted in a semi-shrug that told me he wasn't convinced. That, and the look in his eyes, was leading me to believe this could be an even bigger situation than what I originally thought when I first received his call. He didn't want the mainstream media to get wind of the incidents, but why?

"What changed your mind... about contacting me?"

He leaned forward to explain, but he was interrupted when Gertrude rushed into the office with her face flushed with excitement.

"Sheriff, I'm sorry to intrude, but I think the dog... you know, the one whose owner was killed this morning. He or she has been found."

Sheriff Chase raised her eyebrows in surprise. "That was quick. Is he or she okay?"

Gertrude nodded. "Oh yes, she's okay. Agitated, and putting up a fuss, but okay. A customer found the dog when he was at the hardware store. Seeing as the deputies are otherwise engaged at the crime scene, you're all that's left."

***

In small towns like Whispering Oak, neighbors look out for each other, with some saying it was too much, at times, and made them feel as if they lost the privacy they were seeking. If a weather disaster hit the area, they would knock on doors and make sure the residents inside were okay and offer a helping hand if they were not, especially when the heavy snow season hit. If one of them got ill, others dropped off meals and asked if they had any errands to run. It was also a pet-friendly town, with most establishments allowing owners to bring their dogs with them. Others paid attention when a pet was in distress, which is why the sheriff's office got the call so quickly.

Sheriff Chase spent a few more minutes chatting with Gertrude to get all the details, and then she rolled her leather chair back and stood up to go. "Mackie, you mentioned earlier that you knew the gentleman who was killed. Does that mean you know his dog, too?"

Mackie nodded. "The dog's name is Lucy, and yes, she knows me. Jerry—the man who died—used to walk her and sit on my porch for a spell before walking her back home."

"I could use the help if you're up for a ride. We can finish up our conversation along the way."

Mackie glanced toward me.

I shrugged. "I've got the time."

The three of us loaded ourselves into the Sheriff's SUV; Mackie in the front passenger seat, me in the back.

"So, who found the dog?" I asked as we pulled out of the parking lot.

"A customer at the local hardware store heard the dog's non-stop barking. When he went around the back of the store to have a look, he said the dog was agitated and seemed to be focused on a dumpster in the parking lot. He saw the expensive name tag and assumed she just got loose. He tried to comfort the dog while phoning the number on the tag. The call went unanswered, so he called us."

"Poor dog is probably terrified." I thought of Bailey and how she would react if something happened to me.

Sheriff nodded. "I'm sure. Been a busy morning in our little town," she said, glancing over at Mackie. "Which reminds me; you were filling me in on what happened at your home and why you finally decided to inform me."

Mackie turned his head to meet her stare. "Well, Katie and I agree. Knowing this is a small town where the biggest issue you've had to deal with since moving here from New York was a meth lab up in the hills, I'd say Jerry's death is related."

She looked contemplative for a moment, but then surprised. "You think he saw them and they killed him?"

Mackie stared at her. "If I was a betting man."

"Damn Mackie, what was in those cabinets worth killing over?"

Mackie got quiet and his eyes returned to looking out the passenger window.

"That's what he hired me to find out," I said, covering for his sudden silence, but also making another mental note. I remembered his evasiveness when we were going over the items taken and noted that there was something inside those cabinets that he wasn't ready to talk about.

"Some of those items were gifts from my father."

Sheriff Chase looked at me through her rear-view mirror.

"Well, look, I have nothing against private investigators. In fact, we used them as consultants from time to time when I was with the NYPD. But this is my jurisdiction and I've got a crew of selectmen to answer to, and yes, the media if they get involved, so I would appreciate it if we could work together, so to speak."

Before answering, I thought about it. During my last two cases, I worked with law enforcement. Things worked out when I didn't share everything with them. Of course, I knew them. I could tell by Mackie's body language that he wasn't that eager, but it wouldn't hurt. I didn't have to confide everything I discovered to her. She would do the same thing to me.

"Sure, why not?" I finally said after a few seconds of contemplating the pros and cons. I could tell from the way Uncle Mackie's shoulders sagged he wasn't all that pleased.

"It was the media I was trying to avoid," he said with a voice that didn't bother to hide his displeasure.

The sheriff scoffed at him, ignoring his demeanor. "I worked with the NYPD; you don't think I know how to be discreet, and when to keep my mouth shut?"

"No disrespect, sheriff, but it's in your best interest to do so," he added.

She gave him a hard look.

Studying his reaction and body language, I suddenly had the feeling we were going to need more than discretion on this one.

CHAPTER 5 - KATIE

I LEARNED FROM earlier visits with my dad and Uncle Mackie that law enforcement issues were handled by the county in Whispering Oak. The sheriff was an elected position who answered to the town's selectmen. Their office is on the outskirts of town. There are three deputies for each shift, an in-house crime scene tech, and Gertrude handles all the office administrative duties. The Medical Examiner works one county over.

As it was described to me, the sheriff is always on call, takes the reins in most instances, and only signs a scene over to the deputies after the heavy lifting is done. She was the original officer on the scene when Mackie phoned in the dead body. Once she was sure the evidence had been collected and secured properly, and the ME took charge of the body; she had returned to the office after getting Mackie's statement to handle the bureaucracy aspect of setting the case up.

That's why she ended up on the call to retrieve the dog. The two deputies on shift were still at the crime scene. A third one was tending to a homeowner with water in the basement, even though it hadn't rained for days. When we left the sheriff's office, Gertrude was cleaning the coffee machine and microwave that took up the counter space in their small kitchen, with an earpiece in her ear to listen for calls.

"So, how'd you end up in this rural town all the way from New York?" I asked when we were sitting at a red light waiting for a senior citizen's bus to drop off its passengers at the local library.

Sheriff Chase smiled at me through the mirror, but I could also see sadness in her eyes. "Long story, so I'll make it short. I moved up the ranks and joined a gang task force hoping to make a difference in the lives of New York teens being pressured into joining, and wound up having my family targeted by a vicious leader who made his warning clear by killing the father of one of those children I tried to save."

"Oh wow, I'm sorry to hear that. That must have been hard to uproot your family,"

She shrugged. "Water under the bridge now... my husband and I sold everything we owned, drove across the states, and bought a place in the hills. Mackie is part of the reason I'm now the Sheriff."

She looked at Mackie with fondness. He returned the look with his own genuine smile. "I only made the introductions. It was you who won them over."

"That's quite a change from the big city to small town, Americano. You must have moved here after my father passed."

She nodded. "Yes, I didn't have the pleasure of knowing your dad, but I've heard nothing but good stories about him. See his picture all the time on the wall at the diner."

My eyes went wide. "They have a picture of my father at the diner?"

Mackie swiveled around to look at me. "Hell yes. Your father was a well-liked man in this town."

That made me smile. "I'm sorry you had to leave New York."

She looked contemplative for a moment. "None of the men and women I used to work with on the

57

NYPD gang unit would believe it if they saw me now. I still can't believe it myself. I wanted to make a difference in the lives of the teenagers, and keep them out of the clutches of the gang currently running certain areas of the city."

"Too bad you couldn't just shut them down. The gang, I mean."

She laughed sarcastically. "Every time we took one leader down, another took his place, and some were more violent than their predecessor. It became a vicious cycle."

"What finally forced your hand?"

"The decision was made for me when the father of a child I saved was viciously murdered, with a warning that my family was next. I couldn't just transfer to another department. When you're placed on a list by the head of a gang, there is no expiration date. I talked it over with my husband. He worked remotely, so he could live anywhere. When I saw the ad for a small-town sheriff, I knew the odds were against me."

"That's where I came in," Uncle Mackie gloated.

"How so?" I said, genuinely curious.

Sheriff Chase placed her hand on Uncle Mackie's and squeezed, which told me that was what solidified the bond between them.

"It was an elected position, and I didn't know anyone in Whispering Oak," she continued. "With our savings, the sale of our home, and my husband's job, I knew we'd be covered for a while. The current sheriff, who was retiring from the position, introduced me to Mackie. He was so well liked and respected in the community. Once he put his support behind me, the rest of the town followed."

I reached up and squeezed Uncle Mackie's shoulder. "Any trouble from the gang since you've been here?" I couldn't imagine they just forgot about her.

I could visibly see her frown in the rear-view mirror. "Other than some terrifyingly threatening words and images of the dead father I periodically receive in my old NYPD email address, life here has been blissfully happy, and the town has been so welcoming."

She turned into the parking lot of the hardware store and pulled the vehicle around back. The three of us observed the schnauzer's agitated behavior. We stepped out of the vehicle and warily approached.

"Sheriff Chase," she said, extending her hand to the gentleman who found the dog while observing its behavior. "You called in this lost dog?"

The customer was kneeling down next to the dog, trying to comfort her. We surmised she was female because of the dark pink collar.

"She hasn't stopped barking at the dumpster since I found her," the customer said.

"I see that," Sheriff Chase said, noting the dog's persistent and angry barking.

Mackie motioned toward the customer that he was going to approach. He lowered his hand, let the dog sniff him first, and then he pet her behind the ears. "Hey Lucy, it'll be okay, girl."

"Do you know who the owner is?" the customer asked, concerned.

"Yes, he and Lucy would walk to my house periodically and enjoy a snack on the deck. Didn't you girl?"

Noticing the dog's attention toward the dumpster, Sheriff Chase marched toward it and glanced down at the contents. She never worked with K-9s, but she knew to pay attention when they gave an alert.

Holy shit... gun! What idiot would toss a gun in a dumpster in plain sight?

"Something wrong?" Mackie said.

I remained where I was so that I didn't interfere, but the minute I caught the look on her face, I knew the dog was barking for a reason.

The Sheriff glanced toward the customer who had given over the leash to Mackie. "You think you can hang tight for a few minutes? I'll need to get your statement."

The customer shrugged. "I guess so. Sure."

Sheriff Chase walked back to her vehicle and opened the back tail gate. First, she grabbed a camera, returned to the dumpster, and took several photographs; a few of the exterior making sure the label and location were noted, and then a few more of the contents inside. Back at the SUV, she placed the camera in a black case and wrote a quick summary of the images with date, time, location, and her initials. Then she slipped her hands into a pair of gloves, grabbed an evidence box from her tool case, and booties for her feet. Once she had them on, she hopped up onto the edge of the dumpster and dropped. She balanced the box on the corner edge of the dumpster. Using the ink pen from her pocket, she picked up the gun and studied the model.

Mackie was paying attention too. He gasped at the sight of the weapon. "That's a Sig Sauer P226, a gun taken from my house this morning."

Sheriff Chase and I both looked toward Mackie at the same time. It was hard to tell if he grasped it; but his admission that the gun was his, and that it was found in the dumpster where the missing dog was found, made him a person of interest in the death of his neighbor.

"I need to secure the weapon and preserve any prints."

She unloaded the gun, dropped the magazine in her pocket for now, and verified there was no ammo in the chamber. Then she placed the weapon and the magazine in the cardboard evidence box. She placed the box on the corner edge of the dumpster while she jumped back out. At the back of the SUV, she wrote a case number, the date, time, description of the gun and location where it was discovered, and signed her initials.

After the Sheriff spent a few more minutes with the hardware store customer, getting his statement and identification, Mackie loaded the distraught dog into the SUV and we headed back to the sheriff's office. The atmosphere had changed inside the small department when we returned.

"The discovery of a body has the deputies frazzled," Sheriff Chase said, as if she needed to explain the change in their demeanor. "They normally handle vehicle violations, an occasional domestic disturbance call, and drugs or shoplifting issues."

"Don't forget the meth lab," Mackie said.

"Meth labs?" I said, shivering at the thought.

"Oh yes," she mused. "I discovered the one Mackie is talking about after a store clerk caught a shoplifter stealing a bag full of Sudafed. The man's skeletal appearance and rotted teeth made me suspect an issue. When I pulled up to his home, I was met by two pit-bulls and his identical twin brother, even the rotted teeth, threatening me to stay off the property with his rifle. That gave me probable cause for a warrant. The old barn on the property was being used to cook meth, which the brothers then sold to a gang in the city."

"The view of the mountains is so beautiful it never occurred to me that something like that would go on here, especially in a small town."

"I have the deputies making periodic runs up into the hills, but there have been no new reports. Though I suspect they're just being sneakier since I shut one lab down. This current situation will keep the deputies busy for a while. I just hope the pressure doesn't become too much, especially if the media descends into our peaceful little town."

CHAPTER 6 - KATIE

THERE WERE NO hotels or B and B spots in town, mainly because a major city was less than a half-hour away and several three and four-star hotels were located there. I wanted to be close by, so I opted to check out The Concord, which was a small single-story motel with a dozen rooms, and within a ten-minute drive to Mackie's place. It was in the older area of Whispering Oak, which meant mostly New England Colonial homes built back when the town was first formed, and most of the residents were known as townies.

After I dropped off Mackie and Lucy—he agreed to care for the dog until the man's family came forward to collect her. Then I drove back the way I came. I continued down 1A along the river until I was in the older section. I turned into the lot for the motel and parked near the office, shut off the engine, and grabbed my backpack as I stepped out of the vehicle. There was a brisk chill in the air, but the sky was a vibrant blue behind the leafless branches of the trees, which would turn dark soon now that afternoon was blending into early evening. There was a time when residents in Whispering Oak didn't bother to lock their doors, but those days were gone, just as in all the big cities. I used the key fob to lock the SUV doors and started toward the office.

A woman with a pixie style haircut, bleached and spike with gel in the front, stood just outside the front door smoking a cigarette, dropping its ashes into the metal can. She looked like a neon sign with her lime-green jogging suit and red converse tennis shoes, but I'm not judging, just admiring the balls she had to pull off the colorful attire. I assumed she was the manager, only because there was only one other vehicle in the parking lot, and she stubbed out the cigarette to open the door for me as I approached.

"Looking for a place to stay?" She allowed me to enter and then followed me inside.

"I am." I took in the surroundings. The motel wasn't much to look at, though it was clean, leaving behind a strong smell of bleach which made my eyes water. I hoped that wasn't the case inside the room. I put it out of my mind. I only needed a shower and a bed to sleep. When I take on a case in a new area, I always bring my comforter and air freshener.

You never know what accommodations you'll encounter until you do.

She walked behind the counter and pulled out a form the size of an index card and handed it to me. "How many nights?"

"I'm not sure, yet," I said, noticing there was no computer. "Can I book it for three and then let you know if I need more?"

"That will be fine. This isn't exactly tourist season." She tallied up the amount with the calculator.

I smiled.

"What brings you here?"

"My dad lived here, so just visiting his old pals." That was true, just not the whole truth. She didn't need to hear it from me that Mackie's home was robbed, a man was killed, and his dog was the only witness. Small towns were ripe with those who liked to spread gossip. Tell one neighbor it could be all over town in a flash, causing other homeowners to panic. They would all know soon enough.

"How nice," she said, feigning sincerity. "I'll need a copy of your license. The room is seventy-five a night during the week. The weekend rate is higher if you're still here."

I reached for my wallet and pulled out my license, grabbing a credit card at the same time.

She made a copy of the license and swiped the VISA on a small electric card reader that spit out a printed version for me to sign. She kept the cards until I handed the signed receipt back to her, and then she returned them, along with the plastic key card for room eleven.

When I left the office, she returned to her spot out front and lit another cigarette. I stepped into my SUV, reversed out of the spot, and parked in front of room eleven. There was a Ford truck with an image of the American flag on the left corner of the back window and an ARMY sticker on the right parked in front of room nine. Maybe someone back from Afghanistan and trying to readjust back into the real world or visiting relatives. I slung the backpack over my shoulder, grabbed the duffel with my laptop, comforter and pillow from the back seat, and headed toward the room. Even though I was several rooms away from the office, the cigarette smoke still found its way in my direction.

I slipped the key card into the slot and shoved the door handle down to open it when I saw the green light blink on. Thankfully, the odor of bleach was not as strong when I stepped inside, though the air was musty. The room had two queen beds with flowered bedspreads, a chair in the corner, ugly maroon carpeting and curtains to match, a desk with the standard bible in the drawer, and a flat-screen TV. A small refrigerator and microwave were in the small closet, and the bathroom was standard for motels of that size, with a tub and shower head with the cheap white towels and soap, shampoo, and conditioner in small plastic bottles. It also had an interior door that would open to the next room. I didn't worry about that. I doubted there would be an influx of tourists suddenly needing a place to stay and making The Concord their choice.

I placed the comforter and pillow in the chair, set my duffel on one bed, and pulled my laptop out and placed it on the desk. Then I pulled the bottle of air freshener out of the duffel and sprayed throughout the room and bathroom until the scent of lavender filled my nostrils.

"That's better," I said to myself.

Before doing anything else, I sent texts to Olivia, Madison, and Finn to let them know where I was staying, along with an update on the recent case. I didn't expect a reply from any of them. Olivia and Madison finally went on that cruise they planned, which was interrupted when they were abducted and held captive. Finn was back at work. Once the department cleared him, he'd be back to working undercover, which meant only texting him on a personal cell phone number he gave me. I didn't expect to hear from him too often.

Next, I called Derek to fill him in. "Hey Derek, just checking in," I said when he picked up.

"Talk to me," he said, cutting to the chase. The minute I told him about the call from Uncle Mackie, he was intrigued.

"Uncle Mackie and I agree; we don't think it was a typical burglary. They zeroed in on the cabinets where he kept his military possessions; restored weapons, photographs from his time in Vietnam and Damascus, and the medals dad gave him. They ignored the rest of the house; didn't even go upstairs. If it was about money; why not? Or why choose Uncle Mackie's house? They also found the dead body of a neighbor in the woods across the street. He was shot while walking his dog."

"So what's your gut telling you?"

As the owner of his own security firm with investigators and former military on his payroll, he was suspicious the minute I told him about the break-in after Mackie first called. Now, with a dead body involved, we both knew this was not a benign situation. He was good at guiding me, but he also pushed me to use my own instincts.

"I'd say there was something in those cabinets they didn't want Mackie to have, and whatever it is, they felt it was worth killing over."

"Do you have a list of the items taken?"

"I do."

"Email it to me."

"Will do. How's Bailey?"

He chuckled. "Loretta has her chasing balls out in the yard with my two dogs. The girl loves her tennis balls."

"Yes, she does," I said. That meant she was content and not missing me, which always made me feel better when I had to leave her. For Bailey, Derek's house was like doggie day care. He had a large fenced-in area with a tennis ball-throwing machine, plastic bins filled with dog toys and large water bowls to keep them occupied.

"I'll alert Connie and Roger that you might need their services on this case for background, or anything else that comes up. Just keep us informed. And Katie, stay safe."

"Thank you, Derek."

After disconnecting from the call, I removed my laptop from the bag, plugged the chord into the outlet, and did the same with a small portable printer. The list of items taken from Mackie's house was on my phone, so I inserted its USB into the computer and uploaded the list to a file I labeled Mackie. Then I sent a copy to Derek's email and got to work.

Being thorough, I started by looking up pawn shops in the surrounding areas and called dozens, asking if anyone came in trying to sell or pawn the weapons.

Some guns were not out of the ordinary: the Glock 17 Gen5 9mm; Glock 19 9mm; and the Glock 22 were commonly used by some law enforcement, so I supplied the serial numbers. The Sig Sauer P226 has been accounted for and is in the evidence lockup at the sheriff's office. There were two M16 rifles—the modified version—that Mackie and my father brought back from their time in Vietnam. Apparently, the original M16 was pushed through manufacturing and soldiers discovered the weapon jammed, and Americans were killed needlessly, because of the inadequacy of the weapon in battle. After an investigation by Congress, the weapon and its ammunition were modified. Just before my father passed away, he gave me a list of items he wanted Mackie to have. The M16 was one of them. His

Silver Star Medal was another, but like I said, that was passed along with a personal note that I wasn't privy to. The antique weapons that were stored in the cabinet were rare, modified and redesigned by Mackie himself. As I suspected, none of the pawn shops I called had any of them in their catalog of new items.

On instinct, I pulled up the security camera video that caught someone outside Mackie's driveway. The figure was blurred on the phone, but maybe if I enlarged it on the computer. Once I opened it in my video software, I was disappointed. The image was still blurry, but his height and broad shoulders confirmed he was male. Not that it narrowed down anything, but it was a start.

I leaned back in the wood chair and put my thinking cap on. With inflation and gas prices hitting an all-time high, the crime rate was up in major cities, and could have filtered out to the smaller towns, but we didn't think this was the reason for the theft. The weapons in Mackie's cabinets were valuable, but if monetary value was a reason for the robbery, why not steal other items in the home? Like Mackie said, he had thousands in cash in the safe upstairs. They didn't even attempt to check the second floor, the basement, or even the garage, where Mackie had thousands more in tools. And if the neighbor being shot was related—which I assume it was—why kill over a theft in a small town? I was sticking with our original assessment: they were after something specific, which meant they knew of its existence before entering the home.

I glanced at the list of items again, analyzing it now with the notion that money wasn't their goal.

There were two triangle-shaped glass and wood-framed boxes with a folded American flag inside. Each flag was flown with Mackie to the country where he served. I had one too, given to me to store the flag presented upon my father's death. Those flags had special meaning, but probably not to a would-be thief. Mackie earned a purple heart when he served in Vietnam. The other medals he had inside the cabinet belonged to my father; a purple heart and the Silver Star. I couldn't fathom a reason for those being the target. They were invaluable to my father, Mackie, and the men who served with them during the time, but again, why would a thief want them?

That left the photographs. As far as I could recall, they were old pictures during my dad's time in Vietnam, and the two years he served as a private contractor providing security for members of the CIA and officials working at an American embassy. Some depicted Mackie, my father, and their third friend, Hal Colson, in uniform. I remember other images too, but I didn't pay them much attention to have total recall. But if they were the target, the question is; why? Was there something of significance depicted in the photos?

If they were the target, the thief or thieves probably wouldn't be happy to know that I had another set of the photographs, as well as many others, taken during the same time period. After my dad passed away, I couldn't bring myself to get rid of anything, so I boxed everything up, carted them to a local storage facility, and secured them inside a large unit I purchased. The only things not in there were items he wanted his buddies to have.

It was getting dark out, so I thought it was a good time to take a break, look for the photos, and then stop for something to eat. I didn't bother calling Mackie to join me. The sheriff had deputies at his house checking for fingerprints or evidence of the burglary. Plus, I knew he wouldn't want to leave Lucy alone under the circumstances.

I slipped the key card into my back jeans pocket, grabbed my backpack, and threw on my bomber jacket to hide my gun. When I exited the room, I poured a light amount of baby powder on the carpet in front of the door. Finn taught me to do that from now on, so I would know if any unwanted visitors came into my room. If someone opened the door, they would leave footprints in the powder. Even if the intruder discovered the ruse; them trying to brush away the powder so it couldn't be viewed was also a clear sign of entry. The Ford truck was still parked in front of room nine and the light was on inside, but nobody else appeared to be around. The motel manager was not at her ashtray outside, and there were no other visitors in the parking lot. I stepped back into the SUV and headed to the storage facility.

CHAPTER 7 - KATIE

THE STORAGE UNIT was in an industrial area of town, mixed in with a local manufacturing firm. The owner has a home in the area that he visits several times a year, but his primary residence is in a wealthy area of Newton, Massachusetts. His local home is surrounded by ten areas with horse property and a Christmas tree farm run by his handyman who lives in the guest house on the property.

I used the magnetic card to get inside the gate. The facility holds six rows of aluminum, climate-controlled units of various sizes. There was also an area where vehicles, boats, and RVs could be stored. My father's classic Ford truck was parked there, sealed to keep the seasonal elements from damaging its exterior. When he passed away, I knew the house would have to be sold, because I couldn't afford to keep it. I was still married at the time and we were already paying for two homes. The one we lived in, which was close to the fire department where my former husband worked, and the waterfront cottage that we renovated and spent the spring, summer, and fall seasons. After the divorce, I took over the cottage, but it was recently torched—long story—and I was now living in the RV. My college roommate willed her waterfront property to me when she was murdered, but I set that up so victims of a human trafficking ring my friend discovered could stay there during the trial preparations. The timing just didn't work out for me to take on my father's house, but I wasn't giving up the truck.

I pulled in front of the unit, stepped out and unlocked the commercial master lock on the garage door and pulled it up. What I faced was daunting.

The unit was a ten by ten with an eight-foot ceiling, packed to its fullness with just enough space in between rows of boxes for me to squeeze through.

I opened my phone and clicked on the notepad app. When I stored my father's belongings, I made a diagram of the boxes, typed out what each one held and from which rooms, and where they were located inside the unit. When my father was alive, he kept all of his military gear, memorabilia, and photographs in the room he used as an office. Everything from that room was on the left side, centered between the boxes for the living room and kitchen.

Realizing what I was looking for was probably in one a box at the top, I grabbed the ladder and carried it to that section. Referring to my phone again, there were two boxes labeled military photographs PMC— meaning his time as private military contractor—so I lowered them to the ground. Seated on the cement floor, I took the lid off one box and started rifling through the images. My father had tons of photographs during that time in his life.

First, I looked through the photos in the box that matched those stolen from Mackie's cabinets and studied them. Some were just images of the three amigos. As my dad said, that's what everyone called the three friends; him, and Mackie and their buddy Hal. Back then, Hal was given the nickname Slim. Looking at him in the picture, I could see why. They were probably twenty-nine years old when serving as private contractors. Hal was attractive and had a slim waistline with narrow shoulders that made him look like a GQ model. He could have been in the advertisement for new recruits. I hadn't seen him since my dad's funeral, but the last time I did, he was still handsome. Distinguished and fit for a senator at his age; very Richard Gere-ish in *Pretty Woman*.

The next three photographs I viewed I had also seen in Mackie's cabinet, but never paid them much attention. It was during their time in Damascus, Syria. They captured the three amigos, but there was also a young woman in the images. She looked like a local, younger than them, early twenties, maybe. It was hard to tell her age with her flawless skin, and the hijab women were required to wear. They were standing in front of the American embassy, not really posing, but someone captured the images. Hal had his arm draped around her shoulder, though it didn't look like a romantic thing, but more brotherly or protective. Both of her hands were clasped in front of her stomach. I turned the images over to look at the back. All of their first names were noted: Mackie, Donnie, which is what they called my father, Slim, and May, which I assume was her name.

I put those photographs off to the side and rummaged through a few others. Another photograph caught my eye. In it, the three amigos were joined by a fourth private contractor. They appeared to be in work-mode, protecting a couple entering a dark Mercedes. Mackie and my father were at the front of the vehicle, M-4s ready, watching. Hal and the fourth contractor were at the rear. The unknown contractor escorted the female into the car. I looked closer; it was May, only in this one she appeared to be younger than the first set of photos. I turned the image over for confirmation. The names on the back were

Mackie, Donnie, Slim, Tex, and May. They didn't note the man entering the vehicle who appeared with May. I added that image to the ones I set aside. All of them were the same as those taken from Mackie's cabinet, except for the one with the couple stepping into the Mercedes. I couldn't recall ever seeing that image at Mackie's place.

If the photographs in Mackie's cabinets were the targeted objective for the theft at his home, what would be the reason? I glanced through the images again, slower this time. It was the photographs that showed May that I kept going back to. She looked younger in the image where she was being ushered into the vehicle. Was the man her husband? Boyfriend? He looked much older than her, but that wasn't out of the ordinary in those countries; even here, to be honest, especially in the celebrity stratosphere.

Were the private contractors hired to provide security for the couple? If so, was that how she ended up in other pictures with just the three amigos? Something was gnawing at me about that? I gathered them up and placed them in the front pouch of my backpack, intending to ask Mackie about them. My gut was telling me the photos were significant.

I put everything else back in the boxes, loaded them back up into their position, and carried the ladder over to its place. Then I backed out of the unit, pulled the garage door down, and added the lock before hopping back into my SUV.

When I pulled away from the storage facility, my mind was cluttered with thoughts about the photos. What was it about them that had somebody paying professionals—which is what I assumed they were—

to break into a man's home, steal items to make it look like a robbery, but kill someone who might have seen them?

I went back and forth with hypothetical ideas, trying to find some scenario that made sense, but my analysis was cut short by the Sons of Anarchy ringtone on my phone.

"Hey Derek, is everything okay with Bailey?" I said the minute I answered. Derek didn't call me often, and it was usually serious when he did.

"Bailey's good," he said. "I just wanted to alert you that somebody is doing a background on your PI firm, and you, personally."

"How can you tell?"

"As you recall, I had Roger and Connie set firewalls and security monitors. I suspect it has something to do with your case, though we couldn't identify who was doing the search."

"So they know Mackie hired a PI," I said, reviewing our actions from the moment I arrived in Whispering Oak. "I haven't noticed anyone watching or following us, but that doesn't mean they weren't."

"Well, keep your eyes open."

"Will do, thanks Derek."

With his warning, I was suddenly cautious and maybe even a little paranoid. I paid more attention to the surroundings than usual, which is why I was struck by the actions of a vehicle behind me. It was probably about three car-lengths back, but the headlights were off, and it was pretty dark by now. Ordinarily, I wouldn't think anything of it, but there were no other vehicles in the area, and I am a trained investigator. I said that in jest, but the vehicle suddenly showing up with no headlights after

Derek's call got my cackles up. As the vehicle closed the distanced between us, I looked through the rear-view mirror to get a look at the driver. It was too dark to see features, but whoever it was had a baseball cap on with his head lowered. As we got closer to town, the car followed each time I made a turn. I tried looking in the mirror when they made the turn, but the side windows were tinted. There was no way I was returning to the hotel to have whoever it was, know where I was staying, so I drove into the center of town. Even though I was not a frequent visitor to the area, I remembered that there were always people walking along the sidewalk. At the very least, the speed slowed down to twenty mph or less, which would serve two purposes: one, to confirm they were really following me, and two, to see if I could get a better look at the driver.

The minute I turned onto Main Street and saw the speed zone sign, I slowed to follow the rules. They did too, but kept a respectful distance back.

When it was clear they would not be deterred, I picked up my cell phone and called Mackie.

"Uncle Mackie, I'm pulling in your driveway in about ten minutes… I'm coming in hot."

"I'm on it, kid," he said, and we both disconnected.

Uncle Mackie knew what I was talking about from the common phrases between him and my dad. I turned down 1A, crossed over the river. The SUV was still on my tail. When I spotted a red light up at the next intersection, I slowed down and gave the vehicle a chance to catch up. But they hit the brakes instead, and kept at a distance, letting the car idle some ways back instead of pulling up behind me.

When the light turned green, I hesitated. Once it was obvious the vehicle would only move when I did, I continued my trek. Mackie's street was two minutes away, so I sped up. At the intersection, I cut to the left without slowing down and punched the gas going up the street. When I turned right into the driveway, I stomped on the brakes, forcing the vehicle to stop.

Mackie stood on his front lawn, his personal shotgun locked and loaded. When the vehicle was almost in front of his house—seeing him with the gun—their tires spun into a u-turn. The car jumped up and over the curb, and was back on the road again, tires screeching as they sped in the opposite direction.

"Next time I'm puttin' lead in their asses," Uncle Mackie yelled.

CHAPTER 8 - KATIE

"UNCLE MACKIE, YOU and I need to talk," I said as I stepped out of the vehicle and tried to slow down my heart rate. I was pumped with adrenaline.

The look he gave me showed both concern and resignation as he put his gun down to his side, glancing up and down the street to make sure they didn't return.

"I guess it's too much to hope those boys were just out for a joy ride instead of intending to do you harm."

I carried my backpack and the stack of photos up to his porch.

"We were way past that the minute they killed your neighbor. Though I don't think they intended to me harm, but they want to know how much I know, and needed me to know they're watching."

He followed me up the stairs and opened the front door. Lucy ran toward us from the kitchen, barking, but obviously feeling more secure since the last time I saw her. I leaned down to let her sniff me and ruffled the fur behind her ears before joining her new friend, Mackie, who she seemed to latch onto.

He locked the front door once we were both inside and led me down the hall to the kitchen. He set the gun next to the refrigerator; making the assumption he might need it again, and walked toward the stove to stir the contents inside a big pot.

"I have some chili heating. Let's eat while you're chewing me out."

I smirked. "I wouldn't need to chew you out if you leveled with me at the start."

"I apologize for that."

First, he put some food in a bowl for Lucy and filled a second with fresh water. "Sheriff Chase let me into Jerry's house to get her food, leashes, bed, and toys."

I nodded and watched him take care of the dog like she was already a member of his family. And then he grabbed two bowls out of the cupboard and two spoons out of the drawer.

"Will you grab the sour cream and cheddar cheese out of the refrigerator?"

I did as he asked and placed them on the wood lazy-susan he made for the marble porcelain island countertop.

While he spooned chili into a bowl, I lined up the photographs I retrieved from the storage boxes and placed them down on the opposite end of the island. I purposely said nothing; just waited and watched for his reaction.

When he glanced over and noticed them, his eyes went wide with a look of surprise, but I also thought I noticed worry, or fear.

"Tell me about the photos, Uncle Mackie."

He placed a bowl in front of me, offered me a spoon and napkin.

"I didn't realize you had more copies... I thought you would have gotten rid of your father's old things when he passed away."

I shook my head. "I kept everything of my fathers, except the items he willed to you and Hal."

Uncle Mackie placed his own bowl down on the table and let out a heavy sigh as he sat down on a stool. I couldn't tell if it was a sigh of relief or worry, but what he said next answered my question.

"The fact that you have those pictures is not good. You saw what they did to the neighbor, and he was just at the wrong place at the wrong time."

"Now we're getting somewhere," I said, digging into the chili, which is one of my favorite comfort foods.

He smiled at my appreciation of his home-cooked meal.

"When you called me to tell me about the burglary, you knew all along what they were after."

CHAPTER 9 - KATIE

HE SPRINKLED CHEDDAR cheese in his chili and then dropped a spoonful of sour cream. "I knew," he said, but he wouldn't look me in the eye.

I responded with my own heavy sigh. "I don't understand why you felt the need to keep it from me, but we have to get past that and move on. Tell me everything. What is it about these photos that somebody had to burglarize your home to get them, and kill an innocent man who obviously saw their faces while doing so?"

His hazel eyes looked into mine. "I was trying to protect them?"

I met his gaze. "Protect who?"

He dropped his spoon and sat back on his stool. His expression made him look like he aged a few years just sitting here. "Hal, your father, but especially May."

He had my attention now. I, too, dropped my spoon. The thought of food right now disappeared from my mind, even though I was starving. I tried to think logically.

"Okay, my father is gone, so nothing can hurt him anymore, only his memory. But Hal, and May—I assume she's the woman in the photographs?"

Uncle Mackie nodded.

Even though I knew my father had flaws, I still idolized him. I criticized him for not protecting me as a child against the woman I called an evil stepmother, but he asked for my forgiveness later. I didn't give it right away. It took time for me to understand that he was unaware of her behavior, since he was gone from the home most of that time, and I failed to tell him. Ultimately, I gave my forgiveness and advised him to be more selective in his future choices; to which he said there would be no more women in his life. He must have meant it, there never was, other than female friends he met through co-ed sporting events or through his buddies.

He didn't talk too much about his time in service in front of me, and I never pushed. Could this be the reason they were usually tight-lipped around me?

"I don't see any other way for us to deal with this situation, other than you telling me the truth, no matter how much it might negatively impact what I think of my father."

I stared at him and swore I saw a tear fall from his eye, but he swiped it away so fast I thought I must have imagined it.

"I'll tell you as best I can."

That statement gave me pause. I worried he still wouldn't tell me everything, but I would cross the bridge of unknowns when I came to it.

"Hal, your father, and I met May when we were working as private military contractors doing security in Syria. She was the mistress of the Minister of Defense, Jamil Amer, that we were tasked with escorting to and from embassy meetings and functions during talks. A man being married and having a mistress in Syria was not uncommon. There was a fourth guy on this detail. We only knew him as Tex. We didn't associate with him or know much about him, other than that. He didn't try to get along with us, so we returned the attitude, so to speak."

"Was he from the same PMC company?"

He shook his head. "No, he was from another private security firm."

"Anyway, May traveled with the MOD on most of his trips and to various meetings at the embassy, so we talked often. She was a good woman, a little younger than us, and she didn't appear to have any family around. She was learning English, so we quizzed her and helped her pass her tests. You could say we became close—almost like her surrogate brothers—even though the MOD probably wouldn't have approved, if he knew. She would cook for us while he was otherwise engaged. Then we started noticing bruises."

"Bruises?" I said, suddenly uneasy. "She was being abused?"

Mackie nodded. "She tried to hide them with her modest clothing and the hijab scarf she wore every day. Most of them she could cover up, because he was selective with his slaps and whips. But there were a couple times where he lost control and they were visibly noticeable on her face, even though she did her best to hide them with makeup."

"Why couldn't she just leave?"

Mackie stared at me. "She was a woman in a predominantly Muslim country."

By that time I was holding my breath, visualizing the horrific treatment this woman was going through, and imagining what the three men wanted to do to the individual responsible. Yet, they acknowledged they were there on behalf of our country—even though they were private contractors—and the man could merely have them replaced by other contractors, or possibly have them killed.

"What did you do?"

Uncle Mackie bowed his head. "The three of us talked it over. In fact, we had many debates and full-out arguments over what to do. We didn't include Tex in our discussions. He seemed to have an admiration for the MOD, and we didn't trust him. On the morning that May showed up with a broken arm and a body she could barely move, the decision was made for us. We could no longer stand by."

"I could see how that would be a major dilemma."

"Hal came up with the idea. We concocted a scenario where it looked as though May ran away. We pretended to scour the area searching for her, and we kept our mouths shut when we were around Tex. Meanwhile, we hid her and then paid the way for her to be transported to the United States via a cargo ship carrying supplies. As PMCs in the country for some time, we had many connections, good and bad."

"Bad, as in criminals?"

Mackie's look inferred it was best not to ask.

"Hal got her a new identity. May was the name she chose because it was easy since her Syrian name was Maysun. We all agreed to never speak her given name again, not even amongst ourselves. We got her an apartment, a job, opened a bank account, and set up a way for us all to communicate that wouldn't be traced, using emails like the old spy days."

My hand covered my mouth, the shock reverberating through my body. The three men, my father included, smuggled an immigrant into this country. That's why Mackie wouldn't tell me from the start. Hal Colson is a United States Senator, but that was the basis for my next question.

"Uncle Mackie, that was years ago. Could it be Jamil Amer? Do you think he found her? Would he even be looking for her?"

He shook his head and shrugged. "I don't know. He had a wife. It seems far-fetched after all these years."

"Have you spoken to Hal? Do you think the fact that they're—whoever it is—is doing this now, that it might have something to do with his senate seat?"

Again, he shook his head and shrugged. "Katie, after all these years, I just don't know."

"I put a call into Hal and informed him of the theft. He doesn't know any more than we do about who is doing this, or why now. Once he went into politics, he got rid of any photographs or documents from that time. He's also surrounded by security that he pays for, but it's May's safety he's concerned with. Both of us have tried to reach out to her via our normal mode of communication, but we haven't heard from her."

I pointed toward a photograph. "Is this the fourth contractor, Tex, and Jamil Amer—the guy getting into the Mercedes with May?"

Uncle Mackie nodded, clenching his jaw, revealing the anger he still felt toward the individual responsible for harming May.

I was just about to ask for more info on Jamil Amer when I got a chill up my spine, and the old gaze detection radar I had when I was being stalked sent me a signal that we were being watched. Lucy sensed it, too. She started growling.

I turned my head to the right, which gave me a view of the hall. I could see the reflection of light from the living room window. At first, I assumed it was just the streetlights, but then I realized someone was pointing a flashlight toward the window, because it moved.

"Mackie, get your gun," I said, and grabbed mine from the holster at my hip.

He didn't need to be told twice. While he went for his gun, I jumped off the stool, switched off the kitchen and hall lights. Now, I could see it clearly. Somebody was out there and their flashlight kept flicking across the front of the house.

"The sheriff cleared the scene earlier, didn't she?" I wondered if maybe a deputy was still out and about.

"Sheriff cleared the scene, but the tape was still in place."

Following my lead, Mackie crept down the hall. At the front door, he peeked out through the peephole. When he couldn't see anything, he opened his cell phone and viewed the security camera app on his screen.

"Nothing coming up on the cameras," he said. "If anyone is out there, they're not on my property."

I shook my head, frustrated with myself. "Maybe it was just a car going by and the lights hit the window just right?"

Mackie didn't look convinced. He opened the front door and walked outside to make sure the area was clear. He had his gun pointed, hunting for his prey, and swept it from right to left.

I joined him on the porch and studied the terrain.

"You see anyone?"

"No," I said, keeping my eyes glued to the woods across the street, listening for movement since it was too dark to see. Just my imagination running away with me, I guess, though I didn't think so.

He motioned for Lucy to come outside and connected the leash to her collar to let her venture out toward the street. To anyone watching, it was just an innocent move of a new pet owner walking the dog to let her do her business. He was also sending a message that they would not scare him away from his home.

CHAPTER 10 – THE FIXERS

STEFAN AND COLE were holed up in the hills across the street from Mackie's house. It was too dark to see them, but they were there, just hidden by an additional level of protection. Both were lying flat on their bellies, camouflaged by desert ghillie suits. Their car was parked at the end of the road, hidden among the trees in the dark.

"We need to call Mr. Xavier," Cole said.

Stefan glanced toward him. "Why the hell do we have to call him?"

"He said to keep him informed… and you just heard what I did on the recording."

"He also said we needed to keep this situation contained, which means the less who knows about the woman in the pictures, the better."

"You just heard the PI say she had copies and other images as well. This guy, Mackie, gave her some of the background story that Mr. Xavier doesn't want to get out. I think it's pretty safe to say it's not contained."

"Are you prepared to do what's necessary to make sure it is?" Stefan asked him.

Cole clenched his teeth. "I think you and I have a difference of opinion on the term contained. Didn't it occur to you that killing everyone who comes into contact with those pictures just adds another dimension to the story? Dead bodies bring more attention and questions than a few pictures of a woman who could ruin a potential political campaign for one man. Is power that important to Mr. Xavier?"

Stefan grunted. "Is that a legitimate question? Nothing touches you if you have power. Hell, man, people die of natural causes, and have accidents all the time. Nobody bats an eye."

"Shit, they saw the light," Cole said, seeing Mackie and Katie standing on the porch with their weapons aimed. "They know we're out here."

"They don't know we're out here," Stefan said, irritated. "They only suspect."

He retrieved his binoculars, put them up to his eyes, and zoomed in. He watched Mackie sweep the area with his weapon, and he got a good look at the woman who he assumed was the private investigator he hired.

"That PI is a looker. Doesn't look like much of a threat, though. What'd you find out about her?"

"She's the daughter of Mackie's best friend, Donnie, one of the three amigos who served with him in Nam and then in Syria when they were PMCs. He's the one who died."

"How long has she been a PI?"

"Not long from what I could see," Cole said, "but she's handled a couple of cases that got the attention of the media because of the players involved. I'd say that was luck, not skill. What I couldn't find out was who funded her. She was a writer until several months ago. She was married for two decades until she learned a stalker was having an affair with her husband. After more craziness, the marriage ended, her house was torched, and the stalker was dead. Not long after, she opened up shop as a PI in an expensive, but small, beach town on Cape Cod."

"Maybe she has a sugar daddy," Stefan said with a sardonic laugh.

"I'm still searching for more info, but there seems to be a firewall," Cole said.

"Somebody with computer experience then," Stefan said.

"One case she was involved in is headed to trial, which means they're keeping a tight lid on the information and witnesses. Some of the info has already been scrubbed from the internet. Not sure by whom, but yeah, it has to be somebody with computer expertise."

"Okay, they went back inside so they don't know we're out here," Stefan said. "Let's head back to the vehicle and regroup."

"And call Mr. Xavier," Cole said.

Even in the dark, Cole could see the whites of Stefan's eyes when he jeered at him. "Don't make the mistake of assuming Mr. Xavier is more discernible with his decisions on how to handle these issues. He's ruthless. You do not know what he did as a PMC, or what he's capable of. He just can't be involved in the dirty work anymore. Need I remind you of his statement early on: 'dead bodies are inevitable'?"

CHAPTER 11 - KATIE

MACKIE AND I spent another hour or more strategizing on what to do next while finally enjoying the chili, which we had to reheat in the microwave. After, I told him it was getting late and I should head back to the motel.

"And you need to get some rest too," I said. "You're still nursing that cough."

He grunted and dismissed me with a wave. "Don't fuss over a silly old cold."

I shook my head at him. "Stubborn old coot, that's what you are."

To that, he smiled. "That's what your father used to say to me. I miss my buddy."

"Me too, Uncle Mackie."

I grabbed up the photos and stowed them back in my backpack, going back and forth in my head where they would be safer. Mackie's home was already burglarized. What were the odds they'd come back and sweep the place again? I ultimately concluded that the images were safer with me. As far as I knew, they didn't know where I was staying. Not yet, anyway.

I kept my eyes alert on the way through town. Like most small towns, most of the shops and the diner were already closed for the night, considering it was a weeknight. When I came near the motel, I drove past it and circled around several blocks, turning down a few alleys. Once I verified I was not being followed, I turned back around and pulled into the parking lot. The same truck with the army sticker was in front of room nine. But now there was a second car. It was a dark-colored vehicle, but it was parked in the visitor parking area. I didn't see anyone inside. The office appeared to be empty. The lights were out. I assumed the manager was in the back room, possibly watching TV or getting a little shuteye. Doubtful anyone would look for a room at this hour. The motel wasn't off the highway, so not an easy stopover for someone traveling and needing a night's rest. Maybe there was some sort of bell or alarm system that would alert her to a visitor when the door was opened. Either way, all was quiet.

I made one more eye sweep of the area and then I stepped out of my SUV, slipped the backpack over my shoulder, and locked the door. I retrieved the key card from my pocket and slipped it into the door. When the green light blinked, I slowly pushed it open. There were no footprints in the white powder, so I breathed a sigh of relief and entered the room. Inside, I locked the door and chained it. I set my backpack on the nightstand, near the head of the bed, where I would rest my head on the pillow soon. I took off my coat and hung it up on the hanger, was just about to take off my gun belt when somebody knocked on the door—three light taps.

My body froze. I couldn't imagine who would knock at the door at this hour. If it was the bad guys, would they knock? I put my eye to the peephole and looked outside. The man standing on the other side of the door brought an immediate smile to my face.

I unlocked the door, opened it, and rushed toward Finn, comforting my body in his welcomed embrace. "I am so glad to see you."

"Well, this is a pleasant surprise," he teased, trying to hold himself upright from my unexpected reaction, which surprised me too. "You should go away more often."

I laughed and ushered him inside. "It's just been a very long day. I didn't think we'd be seeing each other for a while. What are you doing here?"

He sat down on the end of the bed and pulled me down on top of his lap. "I can't stay long because of the assignment, but wanted to see you before I go dark."

He pulled me to his chest and covered my lips with his, both of us quenching a need. When he released me, he studied my face. "So, tell me about your long day."

I took a deep breath and let it out. "Mackie, Hal, and my father got themselves involved in something back when they were private contractors, and somebody doesn't want the information to get out."

"Is that why they burglarized your friend Mackie's house? Derek has been keeping me updated."

"They also killed a neighbor who was walking in the area. I can only assume he must have seen their faces, and they felt the need to silence him."

Finn raked a hand through his hair and reached for the small bag he brought with him. "That must be why Derek asked me to drop off a file."

"You mean you didn't just come to see me?" I teased, brushing a kiss along the side of his face.

He chuckled. "When I was talking to Derek, he asked if I would be visiting you, and then mentioned he had something for me to drop off if I was. He could have emailed it; but I wanted to see you."

I assumed what Derek sent was important, so I had a quick battle with myself. Either I open the file right away to see what he felt was urgent enough to contact Finn, or enjoy some alone time with him, which might not happen again for a while.

Decision made, I pushed his bag off to the side and placed my hands on both sides of his face. "Right now, it's just you and me. Whatever is in that file can wait until we get reacquainted."

He smiled. "I like how you think." He flopped down on the bed with his head on the pillow, and then he pulled me on top of him. "I'm all yours."

I tried to put Uncle Mackie and his dilemma out of my head; the dead neighbor, and that my father and his friends took part in smuggling an illegal immigrant into the United States. The admission of that, even all those years ago, could be an issue for Senator Hal Colson, even under the extenuating circumstances. But as my lips met Finn's, and I allowed him to sweep me away for a couple of hours, I had a nagging feeling that when I stepped back into reality, I'd discover the smuggling aspect was minor compared to what was really going on. And the burning thought that kept coming up was that this could have something to do with Hal Colson's senate seat, and Mackie was not safe.

CHAPTER 12 - KATIE

I STIRRED AWAKE a few hours later. It took a moment to remember where I was. When I glanced down and realized I was naked with the comforter draped across my legs, a warm glow spread through my body from the memory of two sweaty bodies expressing their feelings. I felt around the bed. Finn's side of the bed was empty. I sat up, thinking he might be in the bathroom.

"Finn?" I called out, but he didn't answer. I pulled the comforter around myself and stumbled out of the bed. That's when I noticed the file folder sitting on the desk with my phone lying on top of it. The screen on the phone showed he left me a text.

"*Morning, babe*," the text said. "*You looked so peaceful. I didn't want to wake you. Had to head out for work. This is the file Derek sent. He said call him if you need Connie and Roger's help. I'll be out of range, so will check in when I can. Be safe, babe. Being with you last night was fantastic. See you soon.*" *Finn xxx*

As much as I wanted to hold on to the emotions that Finn stirred up in me earlier, I knew it was time to get back into game mode. First, I jumped in the shower, and allowed the hot water to wash over me, shampooed and conditioned my hair. I towel-dried off and pulled my hair into a clip to let it air dry. I sprayed some deodorant and body spray, brushed my teeth, and then dressed in clothing optimal for the cooler temps: jeans and a turtleneck sweater.

With my bare feet, I sat cross-legged on the bed, opened the file and read through it. It was all about the life of May Crawford, starting from the date she was smuggled into America until the present. The three amigos set her up in an apartment in Somerville, Massachusetts, where she managed a local coffee chain, similar to Starbucks, but on a smaller scale, with franchises only in New England. She took some personal time off six months later. The report didn't elaborate on why, and then returned two months after that. That made me curious, but I put the thought aside for the moment.

At some point, a local friend moved in with her along with her young daughter, Sierra. After several years managing the shop in Somerville, May saved enough money to buy a small house in Framingham, Massachusetts, and opened a chain coffee shop of her own. Sierra moved to the small house with May, but the other woman—allegedly the child's mother—moved elsewhere.

May's bank account was set up for automatic deposit from the business. She rarely wrote checks, and only used her debit card and paid bills online.

Sierra went to a private school in Framingham all the way through high school and then worked at the coffee shop while going to Framingham State University, where she received a degree in business. Sierra presently helps to run the coffee shop that May purchased and also uses a debit card May provided.

I found the child arrangement with May to be rather unusual, considering she was the child of another woman. Where did the mother go? And why did Sierra have access to May's debit card, instead of one of her own? It was also noteworthy that Derek put an asterisk on that last part, signifying it must be important.

Derek also added a posted note telling me he was currently searching for a background on May during her time in Syria, but that would take some time to work through the international channels.

The next page focused on Hal Colson and his political life. Derek's Intel people offered various reasons and methods of why the discovery of Hal being involved with smuggling May into this country could be used against him in his current position as a United States Senator. It was also noted that if they broke into Mackie's house to steal the images, I should look into whether Hal Colson had any break-ins. Uncle Mackie contacted him already. He didn't mention a break-in, but I thought it might be better if I paid him a visit at some point. Uncle Mackie might feel inclined to protect Hal, which means he would fall on the sword if he had to and keep his name out of it to the authorities. I recalled our chat with Sheriff Chase. He said nothing about the photographs to her. That lead me to believe he could already be in cover-up mode for Senator Colson.

With the death of his neighbor, Mackie saw how far the thieves might go to get their hands on the photographs. That brought up a few questions for me, albeit of a personal nature; how far was Mackie willing to go to keep the secret between himself, Hal Colson, and May, from going public? If it went public, who would suffer from the ˌfallout? Would May be forced to return to Syria, which could put her life at risk by the hands of the individual who had abused her?

Asking myself those questions, I took out my pad of paper and made a list of people I needed to speak to in order to find some answers. I already made note that I should speak with Hal and May. Derek supplied me with enough information to follow up on. I also noted that I should find out the identity of Tex and see if I could find any current info on Jamil Amer. In order to do that, I took a snapshot of the photograph with those two men depicted and texted it to Derek. With all the facial recognition software he provided for Connie and Roger, I was sure they would have better luck than I would, and it would be quicker. I added the info; that Tex was a PMC in Damascus, Syria and the Jamil Amer was the MOD during the three amigos time as PMCs.

Within seconds, Derek texted back: "*I've got Connie working on it. I'll contact you the minute she has anything. Keep in mind, like May's identity in Syria; it could take some time with the International delay. But we're on it.*"

Once I had that squared away, I also sent a text to Mackie telling him I was doing some follow-up work this morning and would be there in the afternoon. I didn't want to tell him what I planned to do. He would suggest he tag along.

I jumped off the bed, put on some socks and my boots. I added some supplies to my backpack—not knowing exactly what I would need—strapped on my gun belt and slipped the gun into the holster. Before heading out the door, I threw on my bomber jacket, added more baby powder to the carpeting in front of the door, and locked it on the way out.

When I stepped outside, the gentleman from room number nine was grabbing a duffel bag from the back of his truck. Even without the army sticker on his vehicle, I pegged him as military. He still had the haircut, which meant he could be home on leave, or was retired from the military and just continued the style. I also noticed the tattoo on his upper right arm, just under the sleeve of his shirt. I couldn't make out the image, but I could see the bottom half of the letters: U.S. Army.

"Good morning," I said, trying to be friendly.

Either he didn't hear me, or he didn't feel like talking. It wasn't until he walked around the driver's side door toward the front of the truck that he acknowledged me. Then he stared at me for a few seconds, almost as if he was stunned that there was anyone else at the motel, even though my SUV was parked there. He gave me a curt nod and then returned to his room.

I shrugged it off and assumed he just wasn't a morning person. I stepped into my SUV and put the address Derek provided in his report for May's coffee shop in Framingham. It should take me just over an hour to get there, depending on the traffic. As I reversed out of the parking spot, I caught him watching me through the rear-view mirror. For a guy who wasn't interested in me when I said good morning, his eyes seemed to be focused on me now as I was leaving.

CHAPTER 13 – THE FIXERS

MR. XAVIER'S NOSTRILS flared, fueled by the anger he felt at the moment for the two men sitting on opposite sides of the laptop during their latest face-time call.

"For a couple of former members of the military, the two of you aren't too bright. When I said I wanted the problem contained, I was hoping you would comprehend that it meant to make sure there was no expansion of said problem. But then again, you were dishonorably discharged for killing innocent civilians, claiming as your excuse that they looked like ISIS. You both earned that discharge."

Stefan ignored his client's words. His own past wasn't any brighter. Otherwise, he wouldn't need their services.

"What are you blaming us for? You told us to break in to the man's house and steal photographs showing a woman you don't want anyone to connect to you. Yet, in your pearls of wisdom, it never occurred to you that this guy Mackie didn't have the only copy of those photographs."

"How the hell was I supposed to know they had copies made?"

"Now, who does not sound too bright?" Stefan mocked in return. "You should have at least considered the possibility when you referred to the men involved as the three amigos. They were tight. You told us that Mackie's best friend who served with him at the time in question had died, suggesting there wouldn't be any other photographs or evidence lying around. You failed to alert us to the fact that he had a daughter. She's the PI Mackie hired, and the one in possession of a second set of photographs."

"I could see how he missed it," Cole said, offering an explanation. "She was married for over twenty years and went by her married name, so he might not have caught it when studying the players during the background phase."

"Oh, so now you're making excuses for him?" Stefan said, frowning. "If he did a thorough search of Donnie Phelps, Mackie's best friend, it would have registered that he had a daughter. Her maiden name would still come up, if he had actually looked. And in case you didn't notice, he insulted you, too."

Cole shrugged. "I'm just saying. Sometimes records get lost when people move out of town."

Stefan leaned back in his seat and crossed his arms over his chest. "Well, instead of hurling insults at us, Mr. Xavier," and he said it in such a snide way that it was obvious how he felt, "maybe you should listen to the latest recording. We discovered another little tidbit that you failed to tell us."

Mr. Xavier's eyes swiveled toward Cole, suddenly deciding he was the one with the common sense in this situation. "What's he talking about?"

Cole retrieved his phone from his pocket, tapped his finger on the recording app on the screen, and clicked play on the clip. It was the recording of the conversation between Mackie and Katie where they discussed the man in the Mercedes, and the other private contractor in one image that Mackie referred to as Tex.

"Fuck!" Mr. Xavier said, slamming his fist down on his mahogany desk. "She actually said she has a photograph with me in it?"

Cole nodded. "She specifically asked Mackie if Tex—that's what she called you—and Jamil Amer were the two men depicted in a picture she has in her possession."

"How could you not know that?" Stefan said. "Did it conveniently slip your mind that you were photographed?"

Mr. Xavier placed his fingers on the bridge of his nose to relieve the pressure in his eyes that always turned into a full-blown migraine. "This changes everything. We need to knock this down."

"When you say knock this down, I need to know what that means, exactly."

Cole nodded. "Same here; we want specifics."

"What do you mean by specifics?" Mr. Xavier said, irritated.

"Stefan and I weren't on the same page with your definition of containment," Cole said, "So it's in our best interest to hear it straight from you on what we are cleared to do."

"Specifically, what you're asking us to do or ordering might be a better term," Stefan added.

"Apparently, you two need things spelled out, so let me be as clear as I can be," Mr. Xavier said. "Right now, the only people aware of this issue are all centered in the small town of Whispering Oak. A town nobody's heard of. Isolate the problem and keep it from spreading outside that perimeter. Use whatever means is necessary and I will repeat it: you need to make sure nothing falls back on me."

"There's something else I need to understand," Stefan said. "You've got the three amigos in the photographs with the woman."

"I can see the photographs," Mr. Xavier said, his irritation revealing itself in his tone of voice. "What's your point?"

"Why are we steering clear of Hal Colson?"

"Use that brain you claim to have," Mr. Xavier said with a smirk. "Hal Colson is currently a United States Senator. He was complicit with helping to smuggle a foreign woman into this country. Illegally, in case it needs to be said. Do you have any idea what that could mean for me?"

For a moment, there was confusion in Stefan's eyes and then it was as if a light-bulb turned on. "If the information goes public, Colson could lose his senate seat."

A look of understanding appeared on Cole's face, followed by a frown. "You prefer the opposite," he said. "If we can contain it, we keep any derogatory information from interfering with your future campaign, but it also affords you with a blackmail opportunity to convince Colson to back your missives."

Stefan smiled. "Bingo. Give the man a hand for pointing out the obvious."

Cole stood up out of the captain's seat where he was sitting and walked toward the refrigerator in the center of the camper van, opened it, and grabbed a bottle of water. "If I am to understand what you're saying," he continued.

Mr. Xavier couldn't see him, since he was face-timing on the computer, but he could still hear him.

Cole paused for a moment, twisted the top off the bottle and took a long swig of the water, somewhat amused at the look Stefan was giving him for keeping them waiting.

"Okay, so Mackie and the PI are the only ones who have knowledge of and have seen the photographs," he continued. "Hal Colson knows about them, but he won't speak about them for fear of ruining his political career and possibly a criminal indictment. If we take care of Mackie and the PI, and subsequently hand the copies off to you, the client, then the problem is contained in your view?"

Mr. Xavier nodded. "Once Mackie and the PI are out of the picture, I can handle Hal Colson with the images that will then be in my possession."

Stefan gave him a look of uncertainty. "What about the sheriff and the woman in the photo? Don't we need to concern ourselves with them? You said the three amigos smuggled the woman into the country. Do you have any further info on her?"

Mr. Xavier's expression was anything but pleasant. "The sheriff is a small-town mentality who thinks this was about a burglary. As far as you know, she knows nothing about the photographs. And don't concern yourself about the woman. She's already being handled."

"What does that mean? She's being handled how?"

Mr. Xavier waved a hand toward the camera as if to dismiss the question. "It means she's in my possession, so there's no need to worry about her. Just take care of our current problem, then I can go public with my announcement and you'll get your last payment."

"And the bonus you agreed to pay for our discretion," Cole reminded him.

Mr. Xavier smirked. "We all know signing the NDA won't solidify your silence."

CHAPTER 14 - KATIE

DRIVING THROUGH THE downtown streets of FRAMINGHAM to May's coffee shop via the directions on my GPS, I immediately realized why she chose the location to open her own business and purchase a home under her alias. It was less than thirty minutes from Boston, a large enough area that she could hide in plain sight with the culturally diverse mix of ethnicities in the area. And with Framingham being the headquarters for the Bose Corporation, Staples, TJ Maxx, along with many other health-related and technology businesses, plus Framingham State University, the thousands who traveled through the area for work and school each day were always in a rush with no time for dozens of questions as they stopped for their daily cup of Joe.

I parked on the street near Concord Square, checked to make sure I was alone. I made sure nobody was following me on my drive to the area and then walked around the block a few times to check things out. It was no-wonder that May's shop was prospering as it was. Aside from coffee being one of the number one businesses these days, her location was dead on. She was two blocks away from Concord Square and on the main street, mixed in with dozens of other retail businesses. The court house, town hall, and municipal buildings were also within walking distance.

I spotted the outdoor canopy for her shop because of the bold colors. The vinyl awning was a dark pink color with cursive gold lettering: *May's Coffee &*

Tea. Since she was part of a franchise, I knew from my earlier research after reading Derek's report that the actual company name was Coffee & Tea. Each franchise owner could add their own name or logo to signify it as their own. Through the front window, I could see several cute tables set up, and an individual at the counter placing an order. I did a quick study of the occupants. One young woman was positioned in the back corner by the window, her laptop in front of her, and earphones on. She could be an employee who opted to work remote, or an author churning out her page-count for the day.

Another table was occupied by a woman with two young children, one of them in a stroller. She could be a mother or the nanny. The child at the table was possibly two or three, nibbling on a pastry and drinking a cup of juice. I smiled to myself. The sugar high will hit her on the trip back home, or shopping, depending on the woman's plan for the day.

An older gentleman, wearing an argyle sweater, who I guessed could be newly retired and trying to pass the time, sat at a third table sipping on his cup of coffee while casually looking out the window. I pegged him the type to enjoy a morning of people watching. The street was busy with individuals of all ages and nationalities rushing to their designated jobs or one of the retail establishments along the street. During warmer weather, I was sure May would have tables set up outside, and the gentleman would spend a few hours enjoying what I would have bet was his favorite past-time.

I walked through the front door and heard a cute little jingle. The customers glanced my way, seemed to study me for a few seconds, and then returned to what they were doing. That led me to believe this was one of their favorite establishments, and they were making sure I was worthy of treading on their turf.

"Good morning," a pleasant voice said from behind the counter.

"Good morning," I responded as I casually walked toward the sound and studied the young woman whose voice I heard.

She was pretty. Too young to be May. Maybe she was the young woman who moved in with May as a baby and was now said to be helping her run the business? I didn't want to put her on the defensive, so I hung back while she finished up with the customer, and studied the food items on the bakery shelf. I don't eat sweets for breakfast, so I glanced up at the decorative menu on the wall.

The customer finished paying and gathered the cardboard tray of items she ordered; I assumed she was picking up coffee for employees she worked with, because she had several. The cute jingle sounded when she walked out the door.

"Can I help you?" the young woman said after she was gone.

I smiled and tried to act nonchalant. But I was struck by the resemblance between her and May. All I had were images of May when she was in her early twenties, but this young woman—whose name tag said Sierra—was almost her spitting image. Derek said another woman moved in with May and brought the child with her. Were they relatives? Did May have a family back in Syria who found out where she was? Or did May contact her family? Derek hadn't completed the background during her time in Syria, so right now, I had no clue. But looking into the eyes of this young woman, it felt like I was looking at May. I quickly returned my eyes to the menu; I didn't want to scare her from the start.

"Very cute place you have here," I said, purposely trying to be vague. I knew I couldn't come right out and ask about May. That could put the woman on the defensive for sure.

"Thank you," she said. "It's not mine, though. I just work here."

"Oh, well, the owner did a great job," I continued. "It's very welcoming and homey."

She smiled. "What can I get you?"

"I'm going to try your white egg omelet and one of your strawberry protein smoothies."

"Excellent choice," she said with a genuine smile. "I lived on those during college."

"Oh, great. Where'd you go to college?"

"Framingham State," she said. "I could work here while attending."

Good work ethic, I thought to myself. I observed her as she reached for a pre-mixed omelet inside a container from a stainless-steel refrigerator, placed it in the microwave, and then put together the contents for the smoothie using fresh ingredients. In less than four minutes, she handed me a tray with my meal and added slices of orange.

"That looks delicious," I said, and truly meant it. I could see why the business had been doing so well, even though it was pretty quiet right now.

"Most of our regulars are already at work," she said, as if she realized what I was thinking. "There is usually a line out the door between seven and eight a.m., and again in the afternoon."

"Ah, that makes sense. It looks like a great place to sit with a laptop."

She motioned toward the woman with earphones and a laptop. "She works remote, but says she gets more done when she's here."

I nodded. "How much do I owe you?"

"Go ahead. Eat it while it's hot," Sierra said. "You can pay after you've finished."

"Thanks."

"I hope you like it," she said, and busied herself with cleaning.

I took a seat at the window and dug in to the omelet. She was right. It was an excellent choice. The white-egg omelet had fresh tomatoes and small bites of spinach, sprinkled with cheddar cheese and bacon bits, and a side of sour cream. While I devoured the meal and enjoyed the fresh smoothie, I retrieved my cell phone and pretended to scroll through messages. Instead, I snapped a few images of Sierra, and sent them off to Derek in a text:

"*This is the young woman running May's coffee shop. She looks like she is related to May. Did you get an ID of the woman who moved in with her and brought a child? Have you discovered any family members from Syria who might have had a daughter? I know you said it takes time when dealing with International, but I'm at the coffee shop right now.*"

I finished my egg, but took my time with the smoothie. A few customers came, ordered, and left. Each time, Sierra welcomed them with each jingle at the door, some she seemed to know from previous visits. Others were new, like me. She was very engaging and offered suggestions to those who were first-time visitors. She was very articulate and

111

friendly. I could tell her education had paid off. I wanted to give Derek time to respond before I paid and attempted to ask a few questions. It was better to be prepared with more knowledge. If he didn't get back to me soon, I would have to phrase my questions so that she wouldn't get suspicious, but her responses could help in finding some answers. Like, where is May? Mackie and Hal had been trying to reach her, but she wasn't answering their emails from the communication system they set up. There was nothing in Sierra's manner that would suggest she was worried, so maybe things were just fine.

While waiting—or stalling to be more accurate—I pretended to be doing a little work of my own. I scrolled through emails and then checked my voicemail messages. I was surprised to receive one from Sheriff Chase. When I opened it, I was immediately worried:

"Have you spoken to Mackie? I sent him emails and text messages last night asking him to drop by the office. When he didn't respond, I phoned him a few times. They went to voicemail. I tried again this morning, still no response. I sent deputies to his house. His truck was in the driveway. When they knocked, they heard the dog barking, but he didn't answer. That was minutes ago. If I don't hear from you, I'm going to assume probable cause to gain entry, fearing he's inside and injured."

CHAPTER 15 - KATIE

SHIT, I UTTERED to myself, immediately worried that something happened, remembering last night when I was there. The feeling that we were being watched and seeing the lights flash across the front of his house. When we went outside and couldn't see or hear anything, we thought it was all clear and chalked it up to my overactive imagination. Should we have explored further?

I slipped my phone back into the pocket of my backpack, grabbed some cash, and picked up the tray to carry it over toward the counter. As much as I wanted to question Sierra right now—which was what I came to do—it would have to wait. Mackie's whereabouts and safety were now my concern. Changing my plan might also give Derek the time to come up with more information so that when I did actually question her, I had pertinent facts.

"Hi Sierra," I said, dropping the tray down onto the counter. "The breakfast was great. Thank you."

She rushed over to join me from where she was wiping down the back counter, cleaning up the leftover remnants of coffee beans.

"I'm so glad you liked it. Like I said, it got me through four years of school." Sensing I was suddenly in a hurry, she handed me the check.

I smiled and handed her a twenty-dollar bill, and slipped a five in the tip jar when she handed me the change. "The owner did a great job with the shop. The food is great, and the ambiance is so warm. I'll be back for sure. Maybe the owner will be in during my next visit and I can tell her how much I enjoyed it."

For the first time, I noticed a crack in Sierra's pleasant demeanor and an overwhelming sadness seemed to reveal itself in her eyes. And just as quick, she seemed to catch on that she was allowing a small glimpse into a troubled world, and forced the feeling aside.

"I hope to see you again soon," she said, only this time I could tell she was faking the smile.

I hated walking out of the coffee shop. Sierra might have expressed herself if I had given her the right prompting. I felt it even more when I noticed she had walked toward the table where I sat and was watching me through the window, with a forlorn look on her face. Part of me wanted to call the sheriff and let her handle whatever was going on with Mackie. But the voice in my head, which I knew was my father, was telling me Sierra could wait. There were more urgent matters to handle at this moment. If I made light of Sheriff Chase's warning and something was going on with Uncle Mackie, I would never forgive myself.

While walking toward my vehicle, I quickly dialed the number to her cell phone, which was the number she called me from.

"Katie," she said the minute she picked up. I could hear the worry in her voice. "I'm standing on Mackie's front porch. Tell me he's okay and I won't break in to his house."

"Break down the door if you have to," I said, pushing down on the gas and putting the phone on speaker. "But keep me on the line so I can hear what's going on."

"Do your thing, boys," she said to the deputies who were there with her.

With the phone on speaker, I could hear their every move. I even heard Lucy barking from inside. I could tell she was agitated. She sounded like she did when she was discovered at the dumpster after her owner had been killed. Then I heard a crashing noise when the door opened; and then another noise from something falling down onto the hardwood floor.

"Oh sorry, Sheriff," a deputy said. "Why would he leave his gun by the door?"

"He had his shotgun out last night at dinner when we thought there was somebody across the street in the woods," I said to the Sheriff.

"Was there?"

"We didn't see or hear anyone when we went outside to check; doesn't mean they weren't."

"Mackie," Sheriff Chase called out inside the house upon entering. "It's Sheriff Chase. We're here to do a wellness check."

I could hear them walking through the house. Lucy stopped barking, so she must have remembered the sheriff from when she was discovered by the dumpster.

"Mackie," another deputy yelled.

"I don't see any sign of trouble," Sheriff Chase said, but her voice didn't sound like she was relieved. "Other than the gun being by the door, the place is meticulously neat. There are no dishes in the sink or in the drainer. But there is also no sign that he brewed coffee this morning, and when I checked at the diner, they said he didn't show up for his morning coffee and breakfast."

I gasped. "Mackie goes to the diner every morning. He's never missed a day since Rosie died."

"That's what they said at the diner. That was another reason I called you concerned. I'm checking the second floor."

I couldn't hear her work boots as she took each step, but I could hear her breathing as it sped up. "Either he didn't sleep in his bed, or he makes it every day."

"He and Rosie were disciplined with their daily routine of chores. The bed being made wouldn't be viewed as a sign. Check his toothbrush."

I heard the distinction between walking on the hardwood floor to when she entered the bathroom and strode across the ceramic tile floor. "I don't have a good feeling about this," she said.

Her voice sounded anxious, which was out of the norm from I'd seen of her so far. "What is it?"

I heard a sound, like that of the vanity doors opening in the bathroom.

"There is no sign of him in the house, but no sign that anything has happened to him either. No blood, nothing thrown around or knocked over. The toothbrush was dry, so he didn't use it this morning. But you say the bed being made doesn't prove that it wasn't slept in last night either."

I went through the timeline of when I left Mackie's house and returned to the motel. Mackie would have cleaned up a little, since he was so meticulous. The family room still had crime scene tape up and the glass from the cabinets was still covering the floor. Mackie might have wanted to watch a little TV to take his mind off of things.

"Check the basement," I finally said.

"He has a full basement?" the sheriff asked. "Does he go down there often?"

"Yes, he and my father used to sit in the old recliners down there to watch sports and their favorite military movies on the large TV when they were renovating the main floor."

I was less than five minutes away and getting more nervous the closer I got.

"Sheriff, I got something in the kitchen," I heard one deputy yell, though his voice sounded muted, because she was still upstairs.

"Hang on," Sheriff Chase said. I heard her closing the vanity and medicine cabinet doors. The footsteps started back through the hall and down the stairs.

I'm not sure why, but something caused me to punch the gas as I was driving through town. The law was at Mackie's house anyway, so driving over the speed limit wasn't an immediate concern. I turned left onto Mackie's street, sped up, and then hit the brakes so I could turn into the driveway.

"What is it?" I heard the sheriff say when she met up with the deputy in the kitchen.

"Do we know if Mackie is a diabetic?"

Hearing that, I hurried out of the vehicle and stormed up the steps and into the house. Sheriff Chase looked at me, surprised to see me, since she was still talking to me on the phone.

"Do you know if Mackie is a diabetic?" she said as she disconnected from the call.

"I heard that question," I said. That's why I ran inside. "No, he is not a diabetic. What did you find?"

The deputy shrugged, as if he wasn't sure what he found. He was standing over the sink with a flashlight pointed down the drain. "Who puts a needle in a garbage disposal?"

"Not Uncle Mackie," I said. "What even made you think to look in there?"

Sheriff motioned toward the deputy. "Katie, this is Deputy Boyd. Boyd, this is Katie, the PI working with Mackie, and a close friend of the family."

"Good to meet you, Deputy Boyd," I said.

"Likewise," he said.

The sheriff and I watched him stick his gloved hand down into the garbage disposal and pull out a mangled hypodermic needle out of the drain.

"I wasn't sure what it was," he said, staring at the object in his hand as if it might bite him. "I saw something shiny in the sink. When whoever put it down the drain and tried to run the disposal, obviously particles flew out."

Seeing that, an immediate feeling of dread settled over me. I glanced toward Sheriff Chase. She must have sensed the same thing I did. I was on her heels as she started toward the basement.

She opened the door and flipped on the light switch. I'm not sure what was going through her mind, but she pulled her gun. Then she cautiously trudged down the steps, keeping the gun out front. The basement was a finished basement with two rooms and a full bathroom. We were now standing in a mud room where Mackie built a massive-sized coat rack and bench from the wood from his walnut tree. That's where they hung the winter and fall coats and scarves. There were drawers that pulled out of the bench for the boots and gloves. Standing in this room, we could hear the TV coming from Mackie's former entertainment room before he renovated the family room.

We didn't know what we were going to find, but seeing a needle in the disposal had us fearing the worst.

Sheriff Chase stood with her gun pointed toward the room and then motioned for me to turn the knob. Once I did, she eased the door open with her foot. She swept her gun from right to left to clear the room. But before she gave me the okay sign, I stuck my head in the door to look inside. That's when I saw Uncle Mackie lying in a recliner. He looked peaceful. *Band of Brothers* was playing on the TV screen. At first glance, he just looked like a man who fell asleep during the show.

But I knew that wasn't what happened. Even if Uncle Mackie fell asleep during the series, he still would have gotten himself up, showered, and kept his morning ritual at the diner.

"Uncle Mackie," I cried. I started towards him, but Sheriff Chase held me back and gave me a look that I understood all too well. I'd been in this situation before, when my college roommate was murdered and they needed to preserve the evidence.

She slipped the gun back in the holster and walked toward Mackie, put her index and middle finger on his next to check for a pulse. Before she said anything, I could tell by the look on her face.

Uncle Mackie was gone.

"I'm sorry, Katie," she said, softly. "And I know you want to come over here right now and touch him, but it is best that you don't. We don't know how he died yet. He could have had heart failure, or some other ailment that we don't know about."

I shook my head before she even completed her sentence. "He had a cough recently, but that's it. He didn't die of a heart attack. You and I both know it. Look for a puncture wound. Like Deputy Boyd said, who puts a needle in the disposal? I would bet whoever did this assumed a small town deputy wouldn't have the wherewithal to look in a disposal until it was too late."

"You're probably right on that, which is why I need to protect the scene until the Medical Examiner can establish the cause and time of death."

I nodded. In my mind, I was already sure it was a homicide. The sheriff thought so too. I could see it in her eyes. But as a law enforcement officer, she needed the ME to confirm. I understood that. I heard her yell for Deputy Boyd, and then put a call into the Medical Examiner's office. When she disconnected from the call, I gathered the ME would be here pretty quick. Mackie was well-known and liked in this town. They wanted to give him the respect and treatment he deserved.

I backed up against the basement wall, slid down until my butt hit the floor, and put my head in my hands. I didn't want to cry in front of the sheriff or her deputy if he joined us, but I couldn't hold back the tears. Mackie was my father's best friend and I couldn't protect him. My dad had always said if Mackie or Hal ever called, I was to do everything I could to help. He must have foreseen something like this happening, knowing what the three amigos did all those years ago—smuggling May into the country—that it could be discovered and possibly used against them.

It was time for me to put the emotions on the back burner, allow my investigative thoughts to do their thing, and find out who was responsible and make them pay.

CHAPTER 16 - KATIE

AS MUCH AS I hated leaving Mackie's house, I agreed with Sheriff Chase that it was probably better if I did. They had their jobs to do, and they didn't need another body walking through their crime scene. We did not know how he died, or when it happened. Was he in the recliner watching the TV, or somewhere else in the house, and then placed in the recliner? According to the sheriff, there didn't seem to be any signs of the latter, but she admitted, she only looked at the service. Once the ME arrived, they would be busy prepping the body for removal. The other deputies, and the one crime scene tech on the sheriff's team, would then go through each room in Mackie's home scouring for any evidence that she might not have seen.

Before I left, I asked the sheriff to look through Mackie's pockets to see if she could find his cell phone. I informed her he had an app on his phone where she could view the footage of the security cameras unless they were disabled. The power was still on, but they could have clipped the wires. When she didn't find it, we assumed the suspect or suspects took it with them. Thankfully, Mackie made sure there was no information regarding May on his regular cell phone. He already explained to me he had a burner phone he used to communicate with Hal, which was in the safe in his room. All of his communications to May, or any discussions that involved May, were done via an old spy method, using emails. They had been using the system since the day they smuggled her into America. After a lengthy conversation with Sheriff Chase, I convinced her to allow me to take the safe with me so I could get the phone and review any other information that I might need. I knew the key was taped underneath the nightstand next to his bed from our conversation discussing the earlier break-in. She only agreed after I gave my word I would make a record of anything I took out, and make sure it was returned after I completed my reviewing process.

We also agreed to have a sit down between the two of us so I could fill her in on the facts Mackie had been withholding from her. Even though we just met, I got the sense that she respected Mackie. If I filled her in on the complete story, I trusted she would honor our request and keep the information from leaking to the media. She was a former NYPD cop. They were used to dealing with the press and knowing when to keep a lid on certain information for the good of the case.

On the way back to the motel, I drove around like I was a lost tourist. I cut down the side streets and circled the area a few times to make sure nobody was following me. I stopped at two convenience stores to pick up some food and drinks; the first one didn't have any wheat or rye bread for the peanut butter and sugar-free jam I purchased. Not the best option for dinner, but since there were no fast-food spots, and I didn't have time to waste in the diner or another restaurant, that was what I chose. Once I felt secure, I turned into the motel parking lot and pulled into the spot in front of my room. Before stepping out of the car, my gut told me I should switch rooms just to be safe. Intent on doing something similar, I stepped out, locked the vehicle, and headed toward the office.

The same manager was on duty at the front desk when I entered, but her attire looked a little more professional; a navy pantsuit, instead of the lime green jogging attire she was wearing when I first arrived.

"You look nice," I said, trying to be pleasant since I would need her help.

"Thank you," she said, raising her head up from the mystery novel she was reading. "We had a staff meeting today. I had to play the part."

I nodded, though I wondered what staff she was referring to. From what I've gathered, she lives in the motel, must be on-call twenty-four hours a day, and I've only seen one maid.

"Are you here to extend your reservation?"

"I am, but I was wondering if you could do me a favor," I said, treading carefully. I didn't want to give her too much information, but enough to where she would go along with my request.

She gave me a look of uncertainty, probably thinking I was going to flake on the rent or something.

"What kind of favor?"

I leaned over the desk as if I was going to confide a dark secret. "I was wondering if you could book me a second room, room twelve, but if anyone comes in or calls looking for me, give them the same room number that I'm staying in now? It would really help me out."

She stared at me for a moment, trying to digest what I was saying. "Are you in trouble with the law?"

I chuckled to myself. That would probably be easier compared to what was going on. "Oh no, it's nothing like that. It's complicated, but I really don't have time to explain."

She took another moment to think it through and then waved a hand through the air. "Say no more. I think I get the gist. We've all had some issues at some points during our lives. But to be clear, you want to pay for both rooms?"

"Yes, both rooms," I said, breathing a sigh of relief. "And thank you for understanding." Though I don't think she really did. She probably thought I was hiding from an abusive boyfriend.

"How many nights?"

"Why don't we make it three more for now?"

"So that's three more nights, and you want to pay for both rooms: eleven and twelve?"

"That would be great. I appreciate it."

I gave her my credit card. She handed it back to me after I signed the receipt. "And remember, if anyone comes in or calls, I'm still in room eleven."

She nodded and winked. "You can count on me. We gals have to stick together."

"That we do."

I walked to room eleven and opened the door with the key card, verified there were no footprints in the baby powder sprinkled by the door. I did a quick walk through just to be sure. So far, so good, but I didn't think my luck was going to hold out too much longer, not after what happened to Mackie. Once I knew the room was empty of someone intent on doing me harm, I returned to the car and grabbed the portable safe from Mackie's house. Inside the room, I used the key fob to lock my vehicle and shut the door. I didn't think anyone was watching me, but if they were, I wanted them to see me enter room eleven.

I never understood why some rooms had connecting doors inside that would open to the next room. I suppose it was good for a family with kids needing two rooms and wanting to have access to both, or maybe it was just necessary for an emergency exit since there was no way out the back, other than the window. I was glad they had it this time. I unlocked the interior door and placed a chair in front of it to keep it open while I switched rooms. I left some personal items behind to make it appear as though I was still in the room. I turned the TV on, but turned the volume low, making sure I could still hear it from the other room. Then I pulled the comforter back on one side of the bed. I positioned the spare pillows from room twelve so that it looked like a person was lying there and pulled the comforter back up. One more sprinkle of powder by the exterior door, and then I pulled the interior door closed and made sure it was locked.

I had no way of knowing if the people who harmed Mackie would pay me a visit, but I would not make it easy for them if they did. They would probably wait until it was dark, so I took advantage of the time and got to work.

First, I made myself a sandwich and then I texted Finn to let him know I changed rooms on the off-chance he showed up. I doubted that would happen though, since he was going dark. I was vague in my words, and didn't mention that Mackie was killed. I didn't want Finn to put himself in jeopardy on the job by worrying. Then I returned the call to Derek. He phoned me when the sheriff and I were discovering Mackie's body, but I let it go to voicemail.

The minute Derek answered, I couldn't stop the emotions. "They killed him, Derek. They murdered Mackie."

"Whoa, slow down," Derek said. "Are you telling me Mackie's dead? When I got your call, you said you were at the coffee shop."

"Yes. The sheriff called me when I was there. She had been trying to contact Mackie since last night, but he didn't return her call. Then he failed to show up at the diner this morning. That has been a ritual of his every morning since his wife died. I rushed back home, but stayed on the line while she searched his house. I got there just as she was headed down to the basement. We found him in one of his recliners, looked like he just fell asleep. But one of her deputies found a hypodermic needle in the drain for the garbage disposal. We assumed foul play. The sheriff will notify me when the ME confirms the cause of death."

"I'm sorry, Katie. I know he was close to your father; how are you holding up?"

"Like I've been here before." I had the same feeling when my college roommate was murdered and the anger that followed. I wanted the individuals who killed her to suffer. This death was worse, since my dad told me Mackie was the reason he lived through Vietnam and could become a father. He always told me it was Mackie's story to tell. Now, I wouldn't be able to ask him.

"Yes, you have been through it before," he said, and he was quiet for a moment. "And I know it would be a waste of time to tell you to come home and let the sheriff handle it. You'll refuse to walk away, even if you think it's too dangerous. Are you locked and loaded?"

I placed my hand on my weapon in the holster to reassure myself. "I am. Right now, I'm more afraid of the anger I'm feeling than what they might attempt to do to me. I'm overwhelmed by a feeling of rage and a sense of responsibility to make them pay."

"That's understandable, Katie. You're the strongest woman I know. Just stay focused and keep your eye on the endgame. Think before you act and don't do something you'll regret. Anything I can do to help, you know I will."

"I know, and thank you." Derek and I have been through so much together in just a few months, but it's been like we've known each other all along. He's become like a second father to me, yet I still know so little about him. Only that he's filthy rich, owns a security company, and has extraordinary connections in both the law enforcement and military communities that are far and wide.

"Okay, so let's get to it," he said. "I sent you what I could find regarding May, the roommate, and Sierra. I think you're looking in the wrong direction, though. Yes, May is the key. But what you need to do is find out who is trying to erase any trace of her."

"Funny you should say that. I'm going to text you another picture. I think the two men in the image could be the key. One of them is the Minster of Defense, Jamil Amer, the man May was connected with in Syria. The second man was a fourth military contractor who worked alongside my father, Mackie, and Hal, but they only knew him by his nickname, Tex. They weren't close, so they didn't trust him.

Mackie couldn't give me any more than that. I plan to meet with Hal, but if Uncle Mackie knew little about the guy, I'm not sure what Hal could offer."

Though he was the one with a protective arm over her shoulder in the images, maybe he knew more.

"Keep in mind he might be evasive once you inform him of Mackie's death, considering his senate seat is at risk."

"And there's that…"

"Okay Katie, send me the pictures you've got and anything else you need me to look into. I'll get Connie and Roger on it right away."

"Thank you, Derek," I said. "You know it's strange, I thought when you convinced me to take on this new life as a PI that I'd be dealing with mostly cheating spouses or missing persons. It never occurred to me I would suddenly be surrounded by death and destruction since I hung that shingle."

"Having regrets?"

I thought about it for several seconds and then smiled at the realization. "Oddly enough, no."

"I didn't think so. Be safe, kiddo," he added, like he always did before he clicked off.

CHAPTER 17 – KATIE

THERE WERE TWO queen beds in room twelve, so I set up my laptop on the one closest to the window. I had the dark cotton curtains closed and kept the room light off, except for the night-light in the bathroom. With the laptop facing the inner wall, I didn't think it would cast too much light into the room if someone in the parking lot was trying to see through the window.

I retrieved the small key I took from Mackie's nightstand out of my pocket and unlocked the safe. My specific reason for needing to see inside was to use his burner phone to contact Hal. If I attempted to call him at his office or home, questions would be asked who I was and why I was calling. Even though it was necessary to inform him of Mackie's death, I knew we still needed to keep it low key. The newspaper in Whispering Oak might get nosey and attach a reporter to the story, but hopefully, we had a little time before it filtered out to the larger media arena. The last thing we needed was a major outlet sending in reporters to dig deeper. I owed it to Mackie, my father, and May—though I hadn't met her yet—to keep it as quiet as I could for as long as I could. I was sure whoever was behind this felt the same; but for different reasons, and they weren't good.

The phone was a used android, Samsung S9 with prepaid minutes and no identity attached. I opened it and typed in the password: Rosie's name and her date of birth. Once it gave me access, I scrolled through the phone log. There was only one number he called religiously, which I knew was another burner phone and only Hal would pick up.

I had to prepare myself for the call. Hal was not as close with Mackie as my father was, but there was still a tight bond between the two men. They served together in Nam, and then the two years as PMCs, going through hell and putting their lives on the line for each other, and their fellow soldiers. They didn't have to see each other often to know the bond between them was never-ending. I recognized the fact that it was so deep Mackie gave his life to keep the secret in order to protect Hal's Senate seat and keep May from harm or being forced back to Syria.

I punched in the number and took a deep breath. My hands were sweating so much from the stress; I had to rub my hands on the comforter. The phone didn't even make it to the second ring before Hal Colson picked up.

"Tell me good news, Mackie. Have you heard anything from May yet? I tried to reach out again, but she's still not responding. Something is wrong. She's never done that."

There was a brief silence as I struggled to find the words. "Hal, it's Katie Parker; Donnie's daughter."

The last time we saw each other was at my father's funeral. We've spoken a few times since then, but usually under better circumstances and the conversations were on his personal cell phone, where a burner phone wasn't necessary to communicate.

"Katie," he said. At first, he sounded happy to hear from me, and then the potential reality obviously hit him and a surge of weariness settled over him. "If you're calling me on this phone… Katie, please tell me Mackie is okay."

This time, I couldn't stop the sudden rush of tears that were now rolling down my cheeks, and it took a few seconds before I could speak.

"Uncle Mackie is gone, Hal."

His breath caught, and I swore I heard him choking up himself. I've never heard a grown man cry, not even my father. Uncle Mackie was quick to wipe away a tear, but Hal's voice sounded more than a little emotional. Because he was in the political arena, he didn't visit my father and Mackie as much; he was elected to do the peoples' business, but they were still the three amigos. It had to be painful to know that he was now the only one still alive after all they went through.

"Damn it Mackie," he finally said after an excruciating silence.

"I'm so sorry," I said, as if it was my fault for not protecting him, even though I didn't have all the facts, or know who to protect him from.

"I'm the one responsible," he said after he pulled himself together and blew his nose. "He was protecting me from something we did years ago."

"I know all about May."

His breath caught again. "Mackie told you?"

I summoned my inner strength. Uncle Mackie was killed because of this mess, but it wasn't finished yet. How far were these people willing to go? Did that mean we were all in danger? Were they seriously going to kill everyone who had knowledge of the pictures? I had to heed Derek's advice and figure out what their goal was.

"I gave him no choice, Hal. An innocent man was killed during the theft at his home. It didn't take a genius to know they were after something other than his restored weapons, flags, and the medals he and my father received during Vietnam. I did my own due diligence and looked through my father's things in storage. The photographs they stole, I had copies, and a couple other images that Mackie didn't realize I had."

The minute I said that, something occurred to me. Whoever broke into Mackie's house got the photographs they were allegedly after. So why would they still be in offense mode? Why was it necessary to kill Uncle Mackie? Unless...

"Hal, can you hold on for a minute? I need to make a quick phone call?"

I realized I was speaking to a United States Senator, and it was pretty brazen of me to ask him to hold, but I only knew him as Hal, one of the three amigos.

"I can do that," he said, almost relieved to have the moment to digest the news.

I placed the burner phone face-down on the comforter so that he couldn't hear my conversation. Then I punched in Sheriff Chase's number on my cell phone.

"Sheriff, are you still at the crime scene in Mackie's house?"

"I am," she responded. "The ME took the body, but we're still here collecting evidence."

"Sheriff, can you take this call outside, please? I wouldn't be asking, but I think it's important."

"Why, what's going on?"

When I didn't immediately respond, I could hear her moving, heard a door open and close. "Okay, I'm outside. Now tell me what's going on."

"Do you have some way to sweep the house for bugging devices? I think somebody has been listening in on mine and Mackie's conversations. And if I'm right, they're listening in on you and the deputies now."

It occurred to me that whoever was calling the shots on this operation were not the same individuals doing the dirty work. If they could kill two people, nothing else was off the table. I had my home bugged once before during a case. I knew these people wouldn't think twice about planting the bugging devices during the robbery. They must have heard the conversation between me and Mackie when I placed copies of photographs out on his kitchen island, and asked him to confirm the identities of the individuals. They know I have other photographs and that I am aware of Jamil Amer and Tex.

CHAPTER 18 – KATIE

IN A SMALL town like Whispering Oak, I doubted the sheriff would have high-tech equipment on hand to check for bugs, but she said she could call in a favor to Springfield PD, which was the closest major city. Until that could be confirmed or denied, she brought the deputies and crime scene tech outside and informed them there would be no more talking. Just silence while combing through the house.

"Thank you for waiting, Hal," I said when I returned to the burner phone.

"Of course." His voice sounded a little more business-like now that he had a moment to think about the situation and his good friend dying.

"I think it's time you and I meet," he said.

"Under the circumstances, I don't think it's a good idea for you to come to Whispering Oak. Can you get away for a few hours tomorrow morning without drawing media attention and make sure you're not being followed?"

"Just tell me where." I could tell he was already planning when the sound was muted, as if he placed his hand over the phone. There were also muted voices in the background that sounded like his private security personnel.

While I was trying to decide on a location, I noticed a document tucked in the sleeve of Mackie's safe. I pulled it out and realized it was a personal legal document between May and the three amigos regarding the coffee shop. I quickly scrolled through it. It said that May Crawford was the individual who managed and was the named owner of the shop. It also showed that it was paid for by silent investors: Hal, Mackie, and my father. I assumed that was another way of helping her keep her identity hidden all those years ago when she wanted to open her own franchise.

To say I was stunned would put it mildly.

"How about we meet at the coffee shop in Framingham that you invested in?" I said; annoyed that this was another part of the story that was withheld from me.

Hal was quiet for a moment. "Katie, I understand that something like this would be very upsetting for you, knowing that we kept it from you all these years? It must feel like a betrayal of sorts. All I can add in our defense is that we thought we were doing the right thing, helping this woman become safe from someone trying to do her harm. After a while, we just knew it had to be kept secret for everyone involved."

"What hurts is that people are dying because of that secret," I said. "I don't know what I would have done all those years ago if I were in your shoes. Maybe the same thing, I don't know. But it's not just about May any more. The photographs are merely pieces of evidence being used for some purpose that we don't know yet, and that's what we need to understand. We also need to find May."

"Is that why you want to meet at the coffee shop?"

"That's one reason," I said. "Uncle Mackie has been trying to reach her through the mode of communication you all set up. He said you've also tried to reach her. If she's not responding, there has to be a reason which makes me concerned."

"You don't think something has happened to her, do you?"

"I think whoever is behind this could have discovered she's living here in the United States, somehow, and they either got to her or terrified her into hiding. I'm hoping Sierra, the young woman currently working there, can shed some light."

"You met Sierra?" he asked, which made me pause. I was told she was the daughter of a former roommate of May's. Hal's question made me curious if there was more.

"Not technically. I was at the coffee shop having breakfast to determine the best way to approach her when I got the call about Mackie. I couldn't question her."

"I hate involving her in this," he said, with what sounded like genuine concern.

"She's already involved as a young woman who has been living with May for all these years, and is now working at her coffee shop."

"I see your point," he acknowledged, but again, I got the feeling there was more. "I've confirmed with my security detail; we can meet you around nine a.m. Will that work for you?"

"That's perfect." Sierra said the regulars were already at work by then. The remote worker might be there, and mothers with their little ones, or the customers hoping to hit the shops along the street. If he had a security detail, I was sure they would enter and scope the place out before the senator walked in.

"See you then," he said. "If there is anything I can do to help with Mackie's arrangements, please let me know."

"Mackie's body is with the Medical Examiner right now while they determine cause of death and a timeline. Once they do, I'm sure the sheriff will contact me. He and Rosie didn't have any children, and as far as I know, his sister is out of state, so she'll have to fly in. I assume Mackie made his wishes known in his Will."

"Yes, he did. He gave me a copy and placed the original in his safe. When we spoke about the Will, he informed me he wanted to be buried in the plot he already purchased next to Rosie. I believe it's at the cemetery near the waterfalls they enjoyed viewing each morning from their usual seat at the diner."

"I'll look for the Will and make sure the sheriff is aware."

"See you tomorrow, Katie."

Once we disconnected from the call, I placed the burner phone back in the safe for now. Folded the real estate document and slipped it back into the sleeve, and looked for the signed Will.

That's when I heard a noise. It sounded like tires running over gravel. My pulse quickened. A vehicle pulled into the parking lot. Other than the manager, the only other person staying at the hotel was the guy in the Ford Truck. He has had no visitors that I had seen, and it was rather late for one to drop in now. I closed the laptop, so that there was no light reflected, grabbed my Smith & Wesson and cell phone, and then walked towards the window and peaked out through the side of the curtain. With no light shining from the inside, they couldn't see me, even if whoever was out there was specifically looking.

CHAPTER 19 – KATIE

THE BREATH I had been holding in escaped with an audible sigh of relief when I noticed it was the Ford Truck pulling back in. But then I had to admit I screwed up, which was not good. I had been so preoccupied with the contents of the safe and the call with Hal that I didn't even notice he left. I needed to be more alert. There was nothing open in town, other than the small convenience store down the street. Maybe he got hungry for a snack. He obviously wasn't the individual I was watching out for, but if he could leave without me noticing, the bad guys could also sneak in and me not be the wiser.

Once the truck was back in its original spot in front of room nine, the motion sensor light went on overhead, and I got a good look at his eyes through the windshield. Strangely enough, he was staring toward the door to room eleven—the room where he thought I was staying. That encouraged me to keep watching, even though I felt like a stalker.

When he stepped out of his truck, he wasn't carrying a bag of groceries or drinks, so I might have been wrong about the convenience store. Though he could have been a smoker buying cigarettes, or one of those individuals addicted to playing the lottery and buying scratch-off tickets. There wasn't too much to do at the late hour on a weeknight in small-town Whispering Oak. Once he shut the truck door, I backed away from the curtain, assuming he was just headed to his room. But he didn't go that way. Instead, he slowly walked toward room eleven, put

139

his ear up to the door, and listened. I was sure he could hear the same thing I did. I had the television set to the *USA* channel, which had been playing *Law and Order* reruns. He raised his hand and looked like he was about to knock. His fist hovered in the air, less than an inch away from the door. But then he suddenly changed his mind and slipped his hand into his pocket. After a few more seconds, he walked back toward his room, unlocked it with his key card, and disappeared inside. I was left to wonder what that was all about.

CHAPTER 20 – THE FIXERS

"MANAGER AT THE Concord Motel said she's still in room eleven," Stefan said, as he disconnected from the call on his cell phone. He pulled the Ram van onto the road and followed the directions showing on the GPS.

"Told you so," Cole said, gloating. "That's what you get for assuming a PI from Cape Cod wouldn't be able to stay too long in a no-tell motel like the one in this small town. Instead of calling around to all the hotels and B and B spots, we should have just camped out nearby. I told you she'd want to stay close."

Stefan gave him a sideways glance. "Doesn't matter who's right. We get all the photographs that she has in her possession, take care of business, and then get the hell out of dodge. I've got plans for that bonus we'll collect."

"Why is it necessary to kill her?" Cole said. "We already got two dead bodies. Why can't we just rough her up to scare her and take the evidence? Without them, there's nothing she can do. She doesn't have all the answers yet, so she's just barking up a tree on what this is all about. Almost the same as we are. You and I both know Xavier is not being completely straight with us."

"What, are you getting a soft spot for this PI?" Stefan scoffed. "What the hell, man? Who cares if Xavier is holding back? The man is a multi-millionaire, considering a run for the highest office. If he wants to hold a few things back that might keep

141

him from running, I'm down with that. Long as I get my check in the end, what the hell do I care?"

Cole shook his head, disappointed in the man he used to serve in the trenches with. Too bad it turned to shit; all for greed and look where they were now. He still cursed himself for the decision he made on that fateful day in Iraq.

It started out like every other day, the two of them in their Humvee checking the area for insurgents. Stefan was all excited and told Cole about a rumor he heard that a hut in the area was being used by insurgents to hide gold they discovered in a mansion from the Saddam Hussein days. Cole tuned him out and said they shouldn't bother getting involved. That it was dangerous. And even if they found the alleged gold, how would they get it back to camp, and then back to the U.S.

But Stefan persisted. And two days later, when they were riding through the area where the rumored hut was located, Stefan pulled the Humvee to the side of the road to watch. After an hour, they spotted three men in the traditional long-sleeved robe they called a dishdasha, loose trousers, and kaffiyehs to cover the heads. They arrived in an old beat up white Toyota truck, common to see during the Iraq war. ISIS traveled in them too.

"That's them," Stefan said, animated over the prospect of finding the gold.

When the men entered the hut, Stefan immediately jumped out and ordered Cole to follow.

Inside, Stefan didn't ask for identification. He raised his weapon and shouted, "Show me your hands and get down on the ground!"

Cole was behind him now, but he didn't have a full view of the three men. His eyes roamed the room, and he saw an AK-47 up against the wall. But before he even registered what was happening, Stefan started shooting and two men were down.

When the third man went to move toward the weapon, Cole raised his own weapon and fired, the bullets entered him from the back. When the man went down, Cole lost control.

"Son-of-a-bitch, Stefan," Cole shouted, freaking out.

"I had no choice, Cole," Stefan said, extremely calm for somebody who just shot two men. "They were going to shoot at me first. You saw them."

That wasn't how Cole saw things, but he couldn't be a hundred percent sure since he didn't have a full view. Still, he didn't think he could rat out his own fellow soldier.

Before he could plan a response, another Humvee rolled up and four more American soldiers rushed inside and took over the scene. It was immediately determined that the three men were not insurgents, but three Iraqi friends who lived in the hut.

When it came time for the inquiry, Stefan said he fired in self-defense, and even though his story wasn't believed, Cole refused to testify against him, saying he didn't have a full view. After all, he went inside the hut, willingly, knowing they were looking for gold. Both of them were immediately issued a dishonorable discharge. The only reason they got off easy was because there was actually gold hidden inside. The three men stole it. The Iraqis agreed with the discharge instead of a trial so they could keep the *story from going public during a time of strife in the war zone.*

And here he was now, Cole thought to himself as he stared out the passenger window, feeling regret. Years later, and he was still following Stefan in another one of his poor decisions. The only difference this time was that he would get paid at the end of this messed up operation.

Stefan eased off the gas as the van slowly drove past the motel parking lot.

"What a fleabag dive," Cole said, seeing the parking lot was mostly empty. "They can't even fill the twelve rooms they've got."

"What did you expect?" Travis smirked. "This part of town is low income, probably a few marijuana or meth dealers hiding inside those two and three-bedroom colonials. It's an old New England town with nothing but a river and waterfall, not exactly a tourist haven. Everything shuts down at nine each night, and they don't even have a package store to buy beer."

"That's why I stocked the refrigerator before we came," Cole said. "I grew up in a small town where nothing ever happened. Why do you think I joined the military?"

Stefan drove around the block a few times, testing the area and watching out for law enforcement, though he wasn't all that concerned. The sheriff and her deputies, who probably never saw a dead body before, were now knee-deep in two murder investigations. He doubted they had the spare time to drive around looking for another potential crime.

He finally found a spot on the street with no parking restrictions that was only two streets over from the motel. The sky was midnight-black. The twinkling diamonds wouldn't be enough light to reveal the two of them sneaking through the back allies dressed in black fatigues, gloves, and balaclavas, armed with guns and knives they stole from Mackie's cabinets.

CHAPTER 21 – KATIE/FIXERS

HEARING A NOISE, I bolted up from where I was lying on the bed. Trying to focus on the sounds, I thought I heard voices. They were trying to whisper, but not doing a very good job at it. It was still dark out—too dark to see inside my room. Somebody was in room eleven. And there went the voices again:

"She isn't here," one voice said.

"She's playing us," a second voice said, sounding a lot angrier than the first.

"Maybe she was expecting us," the first voice said.

So there were two of them.

"That's her vehicle out front. She has to be here."

"Maybe she's in—"

The voice suddenly went quiet, and I assumed it was because they realized I could be listening and decided to use signals instead of talking.

When I grabbed the gun from the nightstand, I felt around on the bed for my phone. I was still dressed in the clothing I had on the day before, even my boots. I expected them to show up. I just didn't think I'd fall asleep waiting for them to make their appearance. After the call with Hal and a quick read of the documents Connie, Derek's computer specialist, sent me, I was emotionally drained. The last thing I remembered reading was the response to my question about May having siblings in Syria. Who was the woman who came to live with May, and why did Sierra remain with May when the woman moved out?

According to Connie's report, May, whose given name in Syria was Maysun Al Numann, was the daughter of a military officer who was killed when she was a young child. She couldn't find any siblings, brother or sisters, but she learned that her mother, Abia, was the housekeeper for the Minster of Defense, Jamil Amer, when May went missing in Syria. At the time of writing the report, there was no confirmation whether her mother was still alive or still worked for the MOD.

If she did, maybe May reached out, and that was how her whereabouts were discovered?

It was the paragraph Connie highlighted in yellow that got my attention: the woman who came to live with May was a nun. She was only at the home with May, temporarily, and the child remained once the nun returned to the church.

The shock I felt after reading that made me understand the situation a lot more. It also confirmed my earlier suspicion and was another piece of the puzzle that Uncle Mackie had withheld. Under the circumstances, I might have done the same thing.

I had to do some quick thinking. The TV in room eleven was still running reruns, so I could still hear the distinct voice of *Olivia Benson*, the female detective on *Law and Order SVU* lecturing her partner, *Elliot*, on his choice of tactics with a perp. I tried to shut out that background noise to listen to what the bad guys were doing. On the other side of the interior door, I could hear one of them. I imagined he was intending to pick the lock to enter, hoping to surprise me. But I also heard what I thought were footsteps outside the exterior door. One of them was out front, probably watching my vehicle.

I thought I knew their goal; get the evidence and take me out of the equation. How they planned to do that was what I didn't know. Would they just shoot me? Did they have silencers to keep the noise down, or was that not a concern for them? They were brazen enough to shoot the elderly man on the street after robbing Mackie's home. And even more brazen, to return to the scene of the crime to kill Mackie. I hadn't heard from the sheriff yet to get confirmation, but I knew they killed him. Even if Deputy Boyd didn't find the hypodermic needle in the disposal drain, I would have suspected foul play.

Either way, I wasn't making things easy for them. My laptop, the photographs, burner phone, other pertinent documents of information on this case, and Mackie's Will, were stuffed in my backpack, which I strapped over my shoulders. The safe was on the bed. There wasn't anything else in there regarding May or Hal Colson, but they didn't know that, so they'd take the time to look or steal it. I also left the duffel bag on the desk. Knowing the photographs were their priority, I knew they'd go for through the bag first, hoping they were inside.

I eased into the bathroom, turned on the shower to make them think I was inside. Walked back out of the bathroom, shut the door and locked it so they'd have to take the time to bust it down. Then, I pulled the curtain aside on the back emergency-exit window; I had pulled the screen off earlier, prepping for my escape. I climbed through and made sure the curtain was closed once I was outside, and then I slid the window shut.

At that same moment, the first man entered through the interior door. A second later, he opened the exterior door and the second man joined him.

"She's in the shower," one of them said.

It would be a matter of minutes now, before they realized I pulled a fast one and was not in the room. And they would be pissed, especially the one with the angry voice. I swear he sounded like the villain in Die Hard. I could visualize him saying to his men: 'Shoot the glass' when McClane was running around Nakatomi Plaza with his bare feet.

The way the motel was situated, there was only one direction which the bad guys could enter and exit from the street unless they were small enough to fit underneath the fence in the back, which led to an alley. I didn't think so if they were former military. I assumed the vehicle they came in would be parked somewhere nearby. They probably assumed the only two guests were sleeping.

Thankfully, I *was* small enough to fit under the fence and could stuff the backpack separately. I hurried down the back alley toward the main street, and crossed over to the other side where I still had a view of the motel, but was completely out of sight. Earlier in the evening, when I was planning this charade of escape, I noticed a spot I could hide in temporarily.

Tucked down low with my eye on the door to room twelve, I debated calling dispatch at the sheriff's office to report intruders with guns. I wasn't sure how fast they'd respond, but I was also concerned about them getting into a shootout with the two men, and it becoming headline news. I called, but instead of going through the dispatch, I asked for a deputy. I didn't want it going out on the scanner. At least I could get some reinforcements, even though it could take a while. If they didn't get here in time, I could at least follow the men on foot. It would be too obvious to go back and get my SUV; they'd be watching for that. Maybe I could get the make and model of their vehicle; a license plate would even be better.

What I didn't expect was that the guy from room nine heard the noise and rushed out of his room brandishing his own gun. He saw the open door to room twelve and entered. The next thing I heard was gunshots.

"Shit!" I said, thinking it was another innocent man who put himself in the crosshairs.

Thinking fast, I looked around for a place to stash the backpack and then slid it off my shoulders. I was just about to run toward the motel and back up the army dude when I saw one man in black race out of the room and run toward the exit.

I didn't hear the sirens in the background, so I had to make a quick decision. Do I go to the room and see what happened to the innocent man, or chase after the perp to get the digits on his vehicle? Fearing the man was injured, or worse, I threw the backpack over my shoulder and ran toward the room. The motel manager was looking outside with a phone connected to her ear when I ran past. I assume she, too, was calling the sheriff. Now it would be on the scanner.

With my gun in front of me, I eased up and hugged the door to room twelve and peered inside. The man from room nine was sitting on the edge of a bed. One hand held a gun that was pointed toward the head of the second man, whose balaclava had been removed. His other hand was applying pressure to a wound that was losing a lot of blood in his stomach, and I was afraid he was going to lose consciousness.

"What's your name, soldier?" I said, hoping to keep him talking.

"Heath, ma'am," he said. "Heath Mitchell."

"Hi Heath, I'm Katie," I said as I eased my hand toward the one of his that was holding the gun. "I'm just going to take the gun and keep watch on this prisoner while you tend to your wound. Is it a gunshot?"

He shook his head. "Got me with a knife. I didn't realize there were two of them."

I took the gun from his hand and watched over the prisoner so he could put both hands on the wound.

The manager arrived at the door just then. Her eyes went wide and her mouth dropped.

"Call for an ambulance," I yelled at her. I don't know what scared her more: seeing the blood from the wound, a man being held at gunpoint, or the terrified sound of my voice. "And then grab a towel and apply it to his wound."

The manager was back to wearing her lime green jogging suit, but I doubted anybody cared at this point. She hesitated, but then did as I asked. While she went into the bathroom, I checked the prisoner for any other weapons.

"His gun is over there on the desk," Heath said.

I glanced toward where he was pointing. It looked like a weapon from Mackie's house, which would give the sheriff the proof that they were the two who had robbed the house.

The manager returned with the towel. Heath positioned himself so she could apply it to the wound and keep her hand in place until help arrived.

I heard a siren in the distance and assumed the sheriff or one of her deputies was finally on the way. I glanced toward the perp, wondering what kind of individual could kill two men in cold blood. He wasn't much to look at, just average looking. Nothing that would show he was a bully, or a man who murdered senselessly. Though, I didn't know which one of them pulled the trigger. As far as I was concerned, they were both guilty. One knowingly pulled the trigger on the elderly man; the other knowingly stood by and watched. And if the sheriff and I were correct, one knowingly plunged a needle into Uncle Mackie's body—the ME to determine where—the other knowingly stood by and watched.

"Are you the stupid one who put the hypodermic needle in the garbage disposal?"

The man maintained a stony expression on his face, but there was a gleam in his eyes like he was having the time of his life.

CHAPTER 22 – KATIE

ONCE THE SHERIFF arrived, the ambulance soon followed. At first, Heath declined a hospital trip, but the Sheriff convinced him that the wound was severe and that he would need several stitches.

"I know you're probably thinking you can just glue it and it will heal on its own, but honestly, the cut is just too wide," I added, along with Sheriff Chase's suggestion.

After a few more seconds of debating, he finally consented and agreed to go with the EMT.

"I'm sorry you were hurt, but thank you for what you did. If not for you, we wouldn't have one man in custody."

He gave me another one of his curt nods, just like he did the other morning. He wasn't much of a conversationalist; I guessed. "Glad I could help. Sounds like they've done some bad things."

I nodded. "You could say that," I responded, knowing I couldn't say too much. "Mind if I check on you when I return from a meeting I have to get to?"

He shrugged. "I'm sure the doctor will tell me to take it easy for a couple of days, so all I'll be doing is sitting in the motel room."

I smiled and waved as the ambulance loaded him into the vehicle and then drove away minutes later.

After Heath was gone, the sheriff and I went over everything that occurred, starting with me asking the manager for a second room, and continuing until I spotted the guest in room nine get engaged in the conflict.

"At that point, I knew I had to return," I told her, feeling guilty that Heath felt he had to get involved.

"When you're through with your meeting, we're going to need to sit down and go over this. What you just told me, I'll need in a written statement. But we also need to go over a few other things that I know Mackie left out."

I nodded. "I will come into your office the minute I finish up in Framingham," I said. "I have a feeling what I learn there will also be pertinent to what you and I discuss."

She raised her eyebrows. "Just who is it you're meeting that is so intertwined in this case that Mackie felt he couldn't confide in me?"

I paused for a moment. It's not that I didn't trust her. I already informed her when Mackie was killed that he was concerned about the media getting involved, so I hoped she took that warning seriously.

"I'm meeting with Senator Hal Colson," I said, and studied her reaction.

It didn't even faze her. "The shit really hit the fan, didn't it?"

I nodded. "Bigger than I knew when I got involved."

She nodded. "I can only imagine. Oh, and by the way; we found two pens with digital voice recording capability in Mackie's house. The house is clean now, though it no longer matters. I'm still waiting on the ME."

So they were listening to everything we said.

After a few more minutes of back and forth, she let me go with the agreement we would meet up later.

Hal Colson would arrive at the coffee shop in two hours, and I wanted to be there early.

Sheriff Chase took the perp into custody. She had enough evidence of what went on at the motel to hold him while she tried to connect him to the break-in and murders. He had one weapon stolen from Mackie's, so that helped, but she still wanted more. Legally, she could keep him for forty-eight hours without charging him, and she wanted to get it right the first time. We both knew the clock was ticking.

Room number twelve was now another designated crime scene, but I needed to prepare for my meeting. Since I was still paying for both rooms, I walked toward eleven. I didn't need to use the key card, because the perps left the door open when they broke in; which had me wondering how they did that. Can you clone key cards?

I needed a quick shower, a change of clothes, and then I had to pack up all my stuff and lock it in the back of the SUV. If the perp who wasn't arrested returned, he wouldn't find anything. I sprinkled white powder on the floor, just to be sure.

***

It was around 8:30, when I sat at a table next to the window with my back to the wall so I could see who came and went. I used extra precautions when driving to the coffee shop, even passing it several times before deciding to park the vehicle and go in. Even with parking, I chose a spot two streets over, knowing I would have to walk the distance going both ways.

When I got in line to place an order, it wasn't Sierra or May, but a young student named Dennis, though he told me everyone called him Denny. After I placed an order for a strawberry smoothie and the white-egg omelet I had on my previous visit, I asked if Sierra took the day off. Thankfully, Denny said she was out running errands and doing the banking, but was expected back in an hour.

I was almost finished with my omelet when I noticed a black Chevy suburban with tinted windows. The vehicle drove by, slowed down almost to a stop, but then continued on. I knew whoever was inside could see out, but I couldn't see in. Still, I knew it was Hal Colson. Five minutes later; the vehicle returned. This time, the right-front passenger stepped out. Even if I wasn't expecting Hal to have his security scope it out beforehand, I would have pegged this man as either private security or secret service. Aside from having buff arms and thighs, he was dressed in a dark suit, white shirt and a light blue tie. That could have described many employees to the businesses in the area, except for his accessories: the mirrored sunglasses and the wire dangling from the earpiece in his ear.

He came inside, did a cursory glance at the customers at the tables. His eyes seemed to linger on me, but then he gave me a curt nod, as if to say he'll be here momentarily. He then walked down the hall where the restrooms were located, verified that they were clear, and returned outside. Once the SUV returned out front, a second security man exited from the back seat behind the driver. The first security man kept his eyes on any threat from the street.

When Hal Colson stepped out of the back passenger seat and slipped his jacket on, he didn't look a day older than the last time I had seen him at my father's funeral. He was blanketed by the two men as they entered the coffee shop. Once he was inside, his ready-made smile was flashing and I noticed him glance toward the counter. My instincts told me he was looking for Sierra. As a Senator, he was on the mainstream media often, asked to respond to something going on in the political world, but I didn't think most of the coffee shop clientele paid attention to that sort of thing. Still, he was ready to shake hands if they recognized him. Once his security pointed in my direction, his affable demeanor changed, and the stress and emotions over Mackie were visible on his face.

When he approached, I stood up and walked into his open arms.

"I'm so glad to see you," he said. "I just wish it was under better circumstances."

"Me too."

He placed both hands on my arms and looked at me. "You still look as lovely as always. I can see your father in your eyes."

I returned to my seat, and he sat down opposite me. One of his security men stood up against the wall behind me. His arms were crossed and his feet wide apart, ready to take on any threat, which made me wonder if threats were a common occurrence for Hal. His second man stood outside by the door to see who came and went. Anyone who noticed would know they were bodyguards or security.

"Is it okay to talk here?" I asked, seeing how he continuously looked around.

"It's as good a place as any. I just hate that it's come to this."

That brought up the question I wanted to ask from the start, but never got around to doing. "Can I be blunt?"

He smiled. "You're Donnie's daughter. I expect nothing less."

"When the three of you, my father included, smuggled May into this country, did you honestly think it would stay a secret for all these years? Were you willing to die or go to jail to keep her hidden?"

Hal looked at me and smiled, as if recalling a memory. "When the three of us debated it all those years ago, those were the questions your father demanded answers to, at first."

He moved his hand across the table, clasped it over mine, and squeezed.

"It obviously concerned us. We argued about the pros and cons for days, and asked ourselves what would happen if the information surfaced. To be honest, by the time we arrived at the point where we were going to go through with it, we had become so sure of our plan that we thought it was foolproof. We were confident that what we did wouldn't be discovered. After what we witnessed, we just couldn't leave Syria when our PMC contracts expired, knowing May could be physically suffering, or possibly even killed. By that time, we decided we would risk it. Remember, you weren't born yet, so we didn't think we had anything to risk."

"Then I guess what we need to determine is why now, and who is behind it. The men who killed Uncle Mackie paid me a visit last night at the motel where I'm staying. No way would they be doing this without some big wig behind the scenes calling the shots. They're just low-level thugs who were possible former military."

"Why do you say they were former military?"

"Because they had enough skill to do surveillance on Mackie's home from a distance," I said. "They cut the power to his security and broke in without detection. They were brazen when smashing the glass on his cabinets to get the goods, which I took to mean they did that deliberately. And honestly, the way they left Uncle Mackie in his recliner, there might not have been an autopsy and it could have been deemed a heart attack or death by natural causes. The reason the sheriff demanded one was because one of her deputies unwittingly discovered a hypodermic needle in the garbage disposal, which gave her cause."

Hal closed his eyes and shook his head, taking a moment to mourn the loss of his friend.

"Uncle Mackie was obviously willing to die to keep the secret. He tried to protect you from anyone knowing your involvement. You need to know that. When he was questioned by the Sheriff, he purposely left the photographs out of the conversation. As of right now, she still does not know they are the catalyst for what's going on."

Hal raised his head and looked at me. I could tell he was back in Senator-mode and I feared he would clam up. But to my surprise, he did the opposite. "Katie, show me what you've got that you need answers to. As I told Mackie, I'm more concerned with May's safety than what might happen to my political career. I appreciate Mackie going to the trouble to protect me, but it stops now. Ask me what you need to and I'll answer what I can."

First, I looked around to verify that the bad guy who was still out there, somewhere, hadn't somehow slipped inside the coffee shop. Of course, I did not know what he looked like, so the move was futile. I opened my backpack, retrieved the yellow envelope where I stashed everything inside, and pulled it all out. First, I did the same thing I did to Mackie. I lined up all the photographs on the table and observed his reaction.

"There was something I didn't think to ask Uncle Mackie. Who took all these photographs of the three of you in Vietnam and then again in Syria?"

"I think it was Grainger," Hal said, trying to recall from all those years ago. "Larry Grainger. You can't see it without a magnifying glass, but his initials are in the lower right corner."

I picked up a photo and squinted, but I couldn't see it.

"Larry was only with us a few months in Nam and wound up with another crew in Syria. He wasn't a PMC. He was a war correspondent. He was always taking our picture and giving us copies. We were still in Syria when he died."

"I'm sorry that he died, but at least we don't have to worry about him being in danger now."

Hal shook his head. "He had cancer."

He smiled after picking up two of the photographs. One of them was an image from Vietnam with just the three amigos depicted. He smiled at the memory. "A person couldn't have better friends than these two men," he said. "They were the real deal."

"My father said if there wasn't a horrific war going on and you hadn't witnessed unspeakable things, Vietnam would have been some of the best years of his life with you two."

His look was somber, but he nodded. "We built a genuine bond during our time there… and in Syria when we were older and more mature. Though that could be questioned right now, knowing what we did."

The second image was the one with the three of them, but May was with them, too. They were in front of the embassy in Damascus. Hal had a protective arm around May. I could tell by his reaction that this picture was significant. I saw the same look on Mackie's face.

"Was that the day you were preparing to hide her and sneak her out of the country?"

His eyes remained on the photo for a moment, and then he looked up and met my eyes. I saw genuine sadness in them. "She was in severe pain in this picture. She had a broken arm that hadn't been treated and bruises and welts were on her body. Before this picture, we knew she was being abused, but it was your father who discovered the severity of her injuries. She was a modest Muslim woman and abided by the traditions, which meant she could hide them."

He pinched the bridge of his nose and took a deep breath. "One day, your father was helping her out of the vehicle. He accidentally touched her arm, and she yelped. He could tell she was physically in pain, but he couldn't ask her in front of the others. So he waited. Later, when the man we were escorting was in a meeting, Donnie approached her. We were all close to her by then, but your dad, well, he just had a way about him. I swear that father of yours could never find a decent woman to stay married to, but with friends, the man had everyone clamoring for his attention."

That brought a temporary smile to my face, because of my own memories of my father.

"Anyway, he somehow convinced her to lower the hijab from around her neck—which by itself could have gotten her in trouble—and we got a look at the damage being done to her. Some were old marks. Some were new. All three of us wanted to murder the son-of-a-bitch."

"If I had been in that situation, I don't know if I would have had the control not to."

"We genuinely feared she wouldn't survive and didn't know another way to save her."

I leaned back in my seat, getting a clearer picture of what these three men did. It wasn't any different from what the men and women who run the underground agencies do to hide women and children from abusive husbands or fathers. Sometimes the law didn't act in the best interests of the abused. The three amigos knew that would be the case for May.

"Back then, Syria was a Muslim country where men had more rights than women. Even though domestic violence was not accepted in Islam, if a woman filed a report against a man, she was rarely believed. Equally, when a man wanted to marry, it was to be decided by the man and the woman's father. May's father died when she was a young child. She would have no say."

"And that brings me to my other question," I said. This time I showed him the picture of the Jamil Amer, the Minister of Defense, getting into the

Mercedes and the fourth contractor who called himself Tex.

Hal's jaw clenched the minute he viewed the photograph, the same as Mackie. I assumed it was because the MOD was the man May was seeing at the time the abuse was happening.

"I have a clearer picture of why the decision was made to bring her here to America. But now, I need to find out who is going to so much trouble to get their hands on these photos, so much that they would kill anyone who viewed them. Could Jamil Amer have discovered her whereabouts?"

When Hal looked at me, he had a confused expression on his face. "You don't know, do you?"

"Know what?"

"Jamil Amer was not the abuser." He placed his finger over the fourth contractor. "He was. His name is Thomas Edwin Xavier, and he's currently considering a run for the highest office in the land. If I came forward to tell the truth about what he did, it's not my senate seat I'm worried about. May will be deported, and all of this," he motioned around to the coffee shop, "it will all be taken away."

It was at that moment that Sierra walked into the coffee shop and the look of recognition on Hal Colson's face confirmed what I had been thinking.

CHAPTER 23 – KATIE

AFTER SAYING GOODBYE to Hal, I gathered the items, returned them to the envelope, and dropped them in my backpack. I wiped down the table so Denny wouldn't have to do too much and walked toward the counter. He was busy chopping fruit and looked surprised to see that I was still around.

"Hi Denny, is Sierra available?"

"Let me check," he said. He set the knife down, wiped the juice from the fruit off his hand, and then disappeared into the back.

When he returned, he also brought another box of strawberries with him. "She'll be out in a minute. Can I get you anything else while you're waiting?"

"No, thanks," I said. "I'm still full from the strawberry smoothie you made for me. So good."

He smiled. "They are, are to die for. We make them fresh every day, instead of pre-made mixes."

Sierra joined us and gave me a nervous smile when she recognized me from the earlier visit.

"You came back?"

"I did. I had to have another one of your smoothies and the white-egg omelet. They were just as good the second time."

"Well, I'm glad," she said, still uneasy. "Denny said you wanted to see me."

I tipped my head to the side, motioning toward a table. "Do you have a minute so I can ask a few questions?"

Her defenses went up. "What about?"

I glanced toward Denny, trying to give her the hint that I didn't want to speak in front of him. She sighed, which I knew meant she didn't want to have this conversation. Somehow, I suspected she had a clue what it was about.

She followed me over to a table with no customers sitting nearby. I didn't have time for small talk or subtle conversation. Sheriff Chase was looking for evidence, and I was trying to protect lives.

"Sierra, I'm a private investigator," I took out my wallet and showed her my ID.

She frowned, as if I tricked her somehow, but then I could tell it was replaced by fear. She looked out the window, and up and down the street, as if she thought we were being watched.

"I was hired by a good friend of mine after his home was burglarized. The thieves were looking for photographs that he had in his possession. They were mages of him, his two buddies, and a woman who they tried to help in Syria many years ago."

Her breath caught, but she tried to cover up her reaction by coughing, as if she had something in throat. She started fidgeting and rubbed her hands up and down her jeans to dry her sweaty palms.

I knew that reaction all too well.

"That friend of mine is now dead."

Her hands covered her mouth in shock.

"I'm sorry to have to say it this way, but there's no other way. I'm worried about May. My friend and his buddy have been trying to reach her, but she hasn't responded."

She placed her head in her hands and started to cry. It was almost as if a dam burst and she let out the floodgates of emotion that she had been holding in. After a few seconds, she was almost inconsolable.

"Sierra, are you okay?" Denny said from behind the counter. "Is that woman upsetting you? Do you want her to leave?"

"She just got some bad news, Denny," I said. "She'll be okay in a minute."

Denny digested what I said, but he didn't completely trust me, so he kept his eyes on us. Each time he sliced a strawberry with the knife, I got the impression he could use it on me if I didn't leave his friend alone.

Sierra finally calmed herself. She walked toward the counter, grabbed a napkin, and then returned to the table. "I'm okay, Denny."

He nodded and accepted her word, reluctantly, but gave me a look that I took to mean: the knife in his hand still had a mind of its own.

"I'm sorry that I had to be so blunt, Sierra. But I really need to talk to May."

She glanced at me, but it looked like she was going to break down again, so I kept quiet to let her speak.

"I don't know where May is," she finally said after a few seconds of silence. "She's missing."

I was afraid that was the case. Mackie said she wasn't responding to his or Hal's messages, and that was not normal.

"When did she go missing?"

Sierra thought about it for a few seconds, as if she was debating how much she should tell me. "She disappeared about a week before you showed up here for the first time. She went out for a morning walk and never returned."

"Did you call the police?"

She shook her head as if the thought of doing so terrified her, and I was pretty sure I knew why.

"You're afraid to call the police because you know she's in the country illegally," I said, and paid close attention to her reaction.

Seeing the fear in her eyes at the possibility of me knowing, I suspected there were no secrets between May and Sierra. When she continued to hesitate, I put my hand over hers. I needed to let her know I was on her side.

"Do you know about the three men who helped May get into the country?"

She didn't know how much she should trust me, but then she slowly nodded. "May told me they were her heroes."

"One of those men was my father," I said. "I want to help."

She looked like she was going to cry again, but this time, it was because she was relieved that the weight of the world was no longer on her shoulders to deal with alone.

"Did you see me here with a man when you arrived?"

She nodded as she blew her nose. "He looked familiar, but I couldn't place him."

"He is one of those men who also helped May. He also wants to help, but he has to do so from behind the scenes. So we have to continue to keep it quiet."

"Can you find her?" Sierra implored.

"I'm going to do my best, but I'll need your help. Can you do that?"

"Of course, just tell me what I need to do."

"First, I need to know the whole truth. Are you May's biological daughter?"

The blood drained from her face. She stared at me for a moment, not knowing what to say. A second later, she stood up and ran down the hall to the bathroom.

The minute I saw her reaction, I worried that I had been wrong about my intuition. If I was right, maybe she was May's daughter, but had never been informed. If that was the case, I just upset her entire world, which made me feel guilty. That was one of the worst ways to find out the truth. And then I felt even worse when I glanced toward Denny and noticed the knife in his hand was slicing the fruit at a high-rate of speed as his eyes glared at me. I shivered at the realization that I made both of them feel so horrible.

CHAPTER 24 – FIXERS

"SIR, WE'VE GOT a problem," Cole said. Several miles away from the center of town, he parked the Ram van at a lookout point on the mountain. He needed to put some distance between himself and the sheriff's station where they were holding Stefan. He drove for a while before he found the spot. It was hunting season, so any pedestrians driving by or walking in the area wouldn't give him a second look. All along on the winding road, he noticed vehicles parked on the side among the trees, their owners walking through the woods with their reflector jackets on, looking for the prey.

He was in the driver's seat, face-timing with Mr. Xavier from the laptop to fill him in on the fiasco this simple operation, as Stefan described it, was turning into.

"Did you get the items and take care of the problem?" Mr. Xavier asked, though his voice was out of character. He sounded rather amused, which Cole found disconcerting.

He was dressed in a dark business suit and tie, but looked rushed, like he had been interrupted and taken away from an important meeting or something. Cole feared that would only add more fuel to his anger once he informed him about what had happened.

"Mackie's been taken care of and nothing should blow back on you," Cole said, hoping that would give him some relief and if what Stefan told him was accurate. This was one time he didn't go into the house with him.

"But no, sir, we didn't get the items. We ran into a complication going after the PI, who we believe is still in possession of them. She somehow slipped out seconds before we raided her room, like she knew we were coming."

Instead of lashing out in anger, Mr. Xavier actually chuckled, which Cole even more unnerved.

"So she's not just a family friend, she actually might know what she's doing. Wasn't her father the one who was the cop?"

"Yes," Cole said tentatively. "Her husband was also a first responder, and the man she's dating a cop. She also wrote books about detectives, so she must have some knowledge and training behind her."

"Meaning, she's more formidable than Stefan let on," Mr. Xavier quipped, almost excited about that prospect. "Why isn't he here communicating that information to me instead of you?"

"That's the complication," Cole said, preparing himself for the tongue-lashing he was sure would follow. "When we were tossing the PI's room in search of the photographs, another guest at the hotel barged in. There was a struggle. Stefan stabbed the guy, but he pulled a gun. I got away before he got the jump on me, too."

Cole braced himself, sure he was going to become the whipping boy since Stefan wasn't around, but all Mr. Xavier did was smirk. He didn't come unglued, as Cole expected. Or maybe what happened was what he expected, because he didn't appear as though the revelation was even a shock to him. In fact, he was rather calm, humored, almost like he already knew. The arrest didn't go out on the scanner, so how would he know?

"What happened to the rules on the battlefield, to never leave your fellow soldier behind?" Mr. Xavier said, trying to work the guilt angle.

"The guy was armed, and he knew how to use it. I think he also had some skills. I didn't think you'd want the sheriff taking both of us to jail."

Xavier went quiet for a moment and Cole thought he noticed a smile on his face, but he quickly dismissed it. "I guess you were the more logical one, after all."

"What do you want me to do, sir? What if Stefan talks?"

Mr. Xavier laughed, but it wasn't maniacal. It was almost as if he was having fun. "Don't you worry about Stefan; like the good soldier he is, he won't talk. He'd die in jail before he'd give me up."

Cole noticed the sudden serious demeanor and the icy tone of his voice. A chill went down his spine, and he couldn't help but wonder if that meant what he thought it did. Was that a threat?

"You're in the big leagues now, Cole," Mr. Xavier said. "Obviously, Stefan can no longer be trusted. He failed the mission and now it's up to you to complete it. Can you get me those photographs and deal with this PI nonsense, or do I need to call in somebody else who I know will get the job done?"

Cole rubbed the back of his neck. The stress over the last few days was nothing like what he felt on the battlefield. There, you knew what to expect. You were fighting against an actual enemy, protecting those you held dear, even though his parents disowned him after he was discharged. They believed he took part in killing three innocent men in Iraq.

Since he refused to testify against Stefan, he had to let them go on thinking that about him.

Yet, as bad as war was, and they went through some horrendous situations, somehow, this operation was making him feel worse. Until the incident that got him discharged, he could rationalize killing for the good of the country. He was having trouble rationalizing what they were doing. It was one thing to break into a man's home to steal photographs that could ultimately harm Mr. Xavier. But the minute he noticed the war medals, and then Stefan killed the innocent neighbor, Cole questioned the mission and his involvement. He would have walked away right then, but he needed the money to get a place and finally have some peace.

He knew that was why Stefan ordered him to wait outside when he went inside to kill Mackie. He didn't trust that Cole would go through with it. The guy, Mackie, was a frigging war hero. Why the hell did he have to die? He felt the same about the PI. Once he got his hands on the photographs, would he have been able to do the deed? He didn't think so.

After a few moments of battling it out in his mind, he had to accept that Thomas Edwin Xavier was giving him no choice. He willingly accepted the assignment because of the money. But now, it came down to survival. It was kill or be killed. As he studied the man currently face-timing him on the phone, he knew that if he didn't take care of the problem, Mr. Xavier would just hire another man to get the job done. Someone who wouldn't care about the brutality, and then he would be on the hit list too. Was he willing to die viciously at the whims of this man? He was starting to believe the man was a psychopath.

The man who thought he could be the future leader of the United States was giving him no way out.

"I'll finish the problem, sir," Cole finally said.

"See that you do," Mr. Xavier said, and then he clicked off without another word.

Before shutting down the laptop, Cole pushed the stop button on the cell phone on the console that he used to record the conversation. Then he shut down the laptop and stowed it in a bag on the passenger seat. Leaning back in the driver's seat, he closed his eyes to think. The last thought he had on his mind before he dozed off to sleep was that the peace he was looking for might be closer than he thought.

CHAPTER 25 - KATIE

I WAITED THE whole time Sierra remained in the bathroom, which was probably close to thirty minutes. I didn't dare approach the counter to ask for anymore snacks or even a glass of water. Denny wouldn't serve me, I knew that. He held me responsible for her being upset. When she walked back out, she was a more than a little nervous. Her eyes darted around the coffee shop, as if she was suddenly in a panic and the bad guys were going to rush into the coffee shop and take her too. When she sat back down, the move was so sudden I could hear the scraping noise from the legs of her wooden chair as it dragged across the laminate floor.

"How do you—"

"Did you know you were May's daughter?"

She nodded.

I glanced toward Denny to see if he was still watching us. Thankfully, he was handling a new customer and neither one of them was paying any attention to us now. I stood up and walked around to stand next to Sierra, and placed a hand on her shoulder.

"It's okay, Sierra," I said, trying to reassure her.

"You don't understand," she said, eyes pleading with me. "If you know, they do too."

I shook my head and urged her back into her seat, but I didn't sit opposite her this time. I sat down next to her.

"They don't know," I said, trying to convince her. "I only know because I have an incredible team

174

behind me. The minute they discovered a nun cared for you as an infant, they took the precautions to make sure that information would no longer see the light of day. I'm the one who figured out that your mother was pregnant when they helped her out of Syria, before it was confirmed."

I pulled the photograph out of the manila folder. It was the one with the three amigos and May. In it, she had both hands on her stomach, while Hal had his arm draped around her shoulders.

"The men who helped your mother get into this country did not tell me May was pregnant. They've continued to keep that secret. It was my intuition. When I learned that a woman with a child came to live with May early on, I remembered this photograph. To me, the image showed a mother already protecting her unborn child."

Sierra's face softened when looking at the image and a tear rolled down her cheek, which she didn't bother to wipe away.

"You look just like her at that age."

I leaned back in the seat and gave her a moment. There was a sudden rush of customers lining up for coffee. Sierra noticed too. She handed the photograph back to me and stood up again. "I need to help Denny."

I stood up too. I grabbed onto one of her hands and squeezed. "Your secret is safe, and I will do everything I can to find out what happened to May."

"Thank you."

I slipped a business card into her hand and the burner phone Mackie used to call Hal. I could easily get another and I memorized Hal's number. I needed her to contact me without worrying about someone listening in. "If you need to get in touch with me or vice versa, here's a burner phone. Do not contact me on the coffee shop phone or on your cell phone."

She nodded, but held in her emotions this time, because the coffee shop was suddenly crowded with customers. Glancing at my watch, I noticed it was getting close to the lunch hour, and Sheriff Chase was probably getting anxious.

***

The hour-long drive back to Whispering Oak turned into two, but gave me the opportunity to digest everything I just learned. And boy, was it a windfall. Knowing what I did now, I took more precautions than usual to make sure I wasn't being followed. I took the back roads and looked like a woman obsessed with porch design ideas and the lush landscaping. I stopped at a few houses and studied the layout of perennials around their yard. Each time, I looked around and verified that nobody got the drop on me. By the time I walked into the station, Sheriff Chase was just about ready to strangle me, or send out her troops in search of me.

For a small station, there was a flurry of activity. Gertrude was busy fielding phone calls and dealing with an individual who I suspected might be the local news reporter. That wasn't good. Once the news of two murders went out on the wire, and a suspect was in custody, it wouldn't be long before others would follow.

I also noticed the deputies were stressed. This was a small town and probably the first time they dealt with one murder, let alone two. I learned how much the locals loved my father after he put up roots here. It was double the support for Mackie, but some of that was because his life was taken from him. Sometimes, there was a morbid curiosity. As a frequent guest to the diner where he would often regale the customers with stories, there was also a bombardment of food being dropped off for the sheriff and deputies working tirelessly to solve the case.

"I'm so sorry it took so long," I said to the sheriff when I entered her office.

"Well, it better be worth my damn time waiting," she said, trying to sound gruff.

"I think it is," I said. I took the seat across from her desk and pulled the folder out for the third time that day.

She cocked her head to the side. "You seem pretty sure of yourself."

"Not so much sure, as much as following my instincts." With a look, I dared her to argue with the reliability of a woman's intuition because I knew she had it, too.

"Before we get to that, you should know the ME informed me of the cause of death. Mackie was definitely murdered."

I leaned back in my seat and sighed after allowing the information to sink in. I didn't say it out loud, but they were going to pay.

"How did they do it?"

"We have to give kudos to Boyd for finding the needle," she said. "The ME said there probably wouldn't have been an autopsy, because of his age, his past medical history showing an earlier heart attack, and that persistent cough we all knew about.

The attempt to destroy the needle in the garbage disposal was the only thing that alerted us to a homicide. Still amazes me that Boyd noticed the particles. I can't see for shit without my glasses."

She handed me the autopsy report. I've only read one other autopsy, and that was taken when my college roommate was murdered. I needed to find out if there were any drugs in her system when she died. There were not, but just as I did then, I did now; I scrolled through all the medical jargon and went straight to the cause of death to read the ME's findings.

"He was injected with insulin?" I looked up at her in surprise.

She nodded. "Injecting insulin in an individual who is not diabetic can cause a hypoglycemic reaction, which ultimately could cause heart failure, which it did in this case. I don't think he suffered."

I lowered my head, taking a moment to mourn the loss of my father's friend, again, but feeling grateful that he went peacefully.

"It's incredible that the ME caught it."

"And again, I applaud Boyd. The ME tested Mackie's blood, urine, and the usual natural substances which showed low sugar. That, along with that earlier find of the hypodermic, caused her to check the body for puncture wounds. If you continue reading the report, you'll see."

I heeded her advice and continued reading. That's when I came to her description: 'A small puncture wound, barely noticeable to the discerning eye, was discovered on his left side, just under his earlobe.'

"Wouldn't they need a prescription to get their hands on that?"

Sheriff Chase shook her head. "No. That's a misnomer. They could have purchased ReliOn insulin at any Walmart without a prescription, only they would have to request it from the pharmacy where they keep it refrigerated."

"So chances are good you can track it down?"

"I've got Boyd calling around to all the Walmart pharmacies in the surrounding area. The prisoner is not talking, so we'll need to cover all the tracks. And even if he decides to chat, it's still better to have all of our ducks in a row."

I handed the autopsy back to her, and we both got quiet. "Okay, let's see what those instincts are telling you," she finally said after a minute of silence.

She rolled her leather chair closer to her desk and leaned over to evaluate the evidence I was laying out. She glanced up and met my eyes. Surprise registered in them the minute I lined up all the photographs.

"Is this Mackie in Vietnam?"

I nodded. "Mackie, my father, and Hal Colson."

"Now Senator Hal Colson," she said, keeping her opinions to herself for the moment while she looked through them all. "And the others are from where?"

"Those images were taken when they were private military contractors in Syria."

After viewing all of them, she leaned back in her chair and appeared to be coming to some sort of conclusion in her head. "These photographs; were they in Mackie's cabinet during the robbery?"

"He had framed copies of some of them in his cabinet."

"Which he purposely failed to tell me," she said, staring at me and wondering why that information was withheld.

I grimaced, but nodded, since I agreed to fill in all the information Mackie left out.

"So let me get this straight," she continued. "Mackie is robbed and some of these photos were taken in said robbery. Instead of contacting me, he called you; a PI?"

"And a friend whose father is also in those images," I added as a reminder.

"Still, he involved a private investigator instead of contacting the sheriff. When you and he came here to admit the break-in after discovery of his neighbor's death, he still didn't advise me of the photographs. That tells me they're significant, which you already know. I'm just coming late to the party."

The manner in which she was discussing the images, I was sure I was going to get a lecture. I worried she might feel compelled to take the photographs as part of the evidence and run her own investigation without me, since I also failed to tell her about them. Thankfully, she didn't do that.

"Let me just remind you; there are already two dead bodies, and it would have been a third, had those two men gotten their hands on you."

That was a sobering thought, which is why she said it. "Thanks for the reminder."

"I'm good like that."

I grinned; at least she had a sense of humor. I hoped that worked in my favor.

"I also just learned this morning that the woman in the photos is missing."

"Missing, as in something, may have also happened to her?"

"I can only speculate."

"So I'm guessing this is the part where you tell me Mackie withheld these photographs, as did you, because you were concerned about the media getting wind of the story and learning of Senator Colson's probable involvement?"

"Not just him," I said. "There are others we were protecting, one of which I only confirmed today. But I am going to trust you with this information because I think you'll do your best to keep the secrets that are necessary."

She studied me. "Meaning you're hoping I will come to the same conclusion as you in determining which parts need to remain quiet."

I nodded. "I trust you will, yes."

She chuckled. "Okay then, lay it on me."

And right then, I got the impression she put on the persona of being tough because it was how she survived working with the NYPD gang unit. Few could handle that gig without some of the ugliness touching them. As a woman, she couldn't show any vulnerability in front of a gang leader she was trying to bust. That would only tarnish her reputation and ensure that they could control her. I suspected that her choice to give up her job in New York was not because she was not good at it or that she was the one afraid. She did so because her husband didn't sign on to be the target of a gang hit squad, and she wanted a better life for the two of them. I understood it, especially after bringing down the sex trafficking club from one of my cases and getting my share of threats. Not to mention the stalker whose actions or brainwashing of a young woman caused the torching of my cottage. Yep, I understood it all too well.

CHAPTER 26 - KATIE

"I REALIZE THERE is a lot to digest," I admitted to her after filling her in on the complete story. I recited everything, start to finish, of what I knew now and I did my best to not leave anything out, starting from when I received the phone call from Uncle Mackie. I observed her reaction each time I added a new piece of the puzzle that she wasn't privy to, but during the entire time I was speaking, I don't even think she blinked.

"That's quite the story," she said, almost as if it was too bizarre to be believed.

"Tell me about it," I said. "It added a whole additional dimension to what I believed about my father; a man who always believed in morality and the rule of law. At first, it was beyond comprehension to hear that he helped to smuggle an illegal into the country all those years ago."

"At first?"

I shrugged. "Now that I know most of the story, I have a better understanding of why they did it. I could even justify it. He used to say the law is the law, but it is not always just. I remember a book he talked about when he was a police officer; *Right to Disobey*, by Kent Greenawalt. My father would recite a sentence that he found profound: '*It is now widely agreed that a person can be morally justified in breaking a law, even a valid law in a democracy whose institutions are by and large just.*' Mackie, Hal, and my father feared that when their PMC contract expired and they had to leave Syria, that

May could have been killed, along with her unborn child. To them, that a man in Syria had more rights and women rarely believed when they complained of abuse was an unjust law."

Sheriff Chase put her hand up to stop me. "But Hal told you it was Tex, the fourth contractor, who was abusing her. He's American."

I nodded. "Except Tex was planning to remain in Syria when they left the country. He signed on to become the personal security for the Minister of Defense after he stepped down from his position."

That didn't sit well with the sheriff. I could see it in her body language. "You've been digging into this; do you know who Tex is and where he is now?"

I nodded. "His name is Thomas Edwin Xavier."

"Holy frigging shit!" Her eyes lit up with recognition.

"Do you know who he is?" I said, stunned by her reaction.

She smirked. "Oh, I know him. And all I can say is this case just got even more convoluted."

"With what you know about him, do you think it's possible that he discovered May was living here in America and found her?"

The look she gave me made me think it could be a lot worse.

"All I can say is May was not the only woman mistreated by Thomas Edwin Xavier."

CHAPTER 27 - KATIE

SHERIFF CHASE PICKED up the phone on her desk. "Gertrude, can you advise the deputy watching the holding cell to place the prisoner into the interrogation room?"

"Will do, Sheriff," she said.

She hung up the phone and then glanced down at the photographs again. "I assume you're allowing me to take these photographs in as evidence?"

I took a few seconds to answer. "Yes, but let me take some snapshots on my cell phone so I have a copy. Not that I don't trust you, but—"

She put her hand up to stop me from continuing my thought. "No, I get it. I also trust my deputies, but I have worked on cases where evidence disappeared before. Do what you need to do."

I opened the camera icon on my phone and took shots of each photograph, and then placed it in an album I labeled Mackie.

Once I was finished, she gathered them up. "I think it's time to have a chat with our guest. You can sit on the other side of the mirror and listen in, if you like, but I can't have you in the room with me during questioning if the case goes to court."

"I understand."

The minute we opened the door, Gertrude was standing on the other side, ready to knock. Her face was the color of ash, and she looked like she'd seen a ghost, or something horrific.

"What is it, Gertrude?" Sheriff Chase said, studying the terrified look on her face.

Right then, we heard a loud noise, then yelling, and a deputy running through another door.

Sheriff Chase didn't wait for Gertrude to respond; she looked too despondent to speak, anyway. The sheriff strode down the hall with me on her heels. Just before she reached the door that would take her out to the dispatch area where Gertrude sat, she opened a door on the left that the deputy went through. I followed her. That's when we saw her youngest deputy standing outside the holding cell with a horrified look on his face. When we reached him, another deputy was inside trying to do chest compressions on the prisoner lying on the floor.

"Shit," Sheriff Chase said, after inspecting the prisoner and seeing the white foam coming around his lips and mouth. "Deputy, you can stop. He's already gone."

"What the hell happened?" I asked, looking around the cell for some kind of weapon, or possibly an item that he could use to strangle himself. How did he kill himself?

"Cyanide," the sheriff said. "He's foaming at the mouth."

"Cyanide?" I started pacing the hall, stunned that this guy was prepared to die. That told me that whoever was paying this guy was prepared to go to hell and back to get what he was after. And it was looking like that guy was Thomas Edwin Xavier.

"Was this prisoner searched when he was brought in to the station?" she asked both deputies.

The young one nodded, almost as afraid of her, suddenly, as he was at what he was seeing on the holding cell floor. Maybe because he feared he made a mistake. "We checked his pockets when we

185

fingerprinted him. He had nothing else, only what he left at the motel room he was trying to rob."

"But he had a visitor just a short while ago," the deputy inside the cell said.

The sheriff and I both turned our heads toward the deputy so fast, I was sure our necks would hurt later.

"Who?"

The deputy shrugged. "He said he was his attorney."

"Except he didn't make his one phone call to an attorney," Sheriff Chase said.

The deputy shrugged. "I was right there with him. I thought nothing of it. Besides, we have cameras."

The sheriff sighed. "Contact the ME's office," she said to Gertrude, who was now standing behind us with her hands covering her mouth. "Tell them I think it was cyanide."

It took Gertrude a minute to register what she said. "Will do, Sheriff," she finally said and hurried back to her desk, though the normal spring in her step was gone.

"Is this what you meant by convoluted?" I said to the sheriff as she ushered me out of yet another crime scene.

"Katie, the gang leader who put out the threat on my family, might be easier to deal with than Thomas Edwin Xavier. With all his money, power, and people at his disposal, you might never know who is coming at you."

"I'm guessing the fact that this is a small town and the deputies aren't used to crimes of this magnitude that it didn't occur to them to keep visitors away?"

She shook her head. "It's like working as interns and having to learn new shit every day. None of them

186

had any experience in law enforcement before they signed on here. And with me as the new sheriff after the original retired, the Selectman didn't give me a choice. Said it was my job to train them. Unfortunately, this mishap falls on me."

While she guided me back toward the cameras, I debated whether the two of us could handle this on our own. Just who was Thomas Edwin Xavier? We know he abused May all those years ago. With the extent of the injuries she sustained over a period, that didn't seem like a man who just flew off the handle over something she did or didn't do. He was a repeat abuser. There were others, I knew it. With all that was going on, I hadn't had the time to check my emails; maybe Derek already sent me a report giving me answers to some questions I was already coming up with.

We came to a door that opened to a small room that was part janitor supplies, with a desk up against one wall that house the computer. Sheriff Chase sat down in the chair and rewound the video to the approximate time the visitor would have arrived.

I stood over her shoulder. Our eyes were glued to the video when an individual walked in and went straight to Gertrude.

"This guy knows what he's doing."

"A professional," she added.

He wore a black suede cowboy hat and boots, a dark suit and tie, but he kept his jacket buttoned, and avoided his face from being seen, both at the front desk, and when the deputy escorted him into the holding cell.

The prisoner was lying on the cot with his hands clasped behind his head, smiling, as if his stay was a pleasant break from the monotony of his day. The deputy opened the cell, and the visitor strode in, and waited until the deputy took a step back.

"Thinking the guy was his lawyer, the deputy couldn't listen in because of attorney-client privilege," Sheriff Chase said.

The alleged attorney sat at the end of the cot. His back was to the camera, so we couldn't even attempt to read his lips. He was only there for less than two minutes. The only change was; the prisoner's smile disappeared from his face seconds before the visitor stood up. When he exited the cell, he mocked us by tipping the cowboy hat to the camera, and then he disappeared with the deputy after he re-locked the door.

"He could have dropped a cyanide capsule on the cot without us seeing it," she said.

She finished up with the security camera. We exited the room and stood outside the door for a moment, both of us probably wondering what move to take next.

"That's three dead individuals because of those photographs," Sheriff Chase said.

I nodded, but my mind was already analyzing other aspects of the case. It was typical of me. I was always trying to find the logical reason things were happening. So far, the only people to know about any of it were in the small town of Whispering Oak, except for Hal, May, and Sierra. Hal was surrounded by security, but even if he wasn't, it would definitely get media coverage if a senator was killed. May was missing. I didn't know if she was dead or not, but I told Sierra I would find out. As far as I could tell, Sierra was only considered an employee at the coffee shop, so I was hoping she was safe. Still, I didn't know how long that would last. Like Derek reminded me, I needed to know the endgame, and fast. I needed my white board, and Finn. He and I were good at working together to find the common denominator. Unfortunately, he was working on his own case.

Deputy Boyd came in through the front office just then, and seeing us, hurried in our direction. "I found it, Sheriff," he said, holding up a slip of paper and his phone.

"What'd you find?" she said.

He stopped in front of her and I realized he was the same diligent deputy who caught the particles in the sink that revealed the needle, so I felt hope. So she had one who seemed to be knowledgeable, or at the very least, did what he could to learn.

"I checked all the Walmart pharmacies in the area, but nothing turned up, so I called several in Springfield. I reasoned they might try a location in the city because there are so many people buying the drug, but they might get lost in the numbers. I was right. A lot of diabetics buy their insulin off the shelf, because it's sometimes cheaper, especially the lower-income families. So I narrowed down the time and day of when the individual would have had to pick it up. Bingo. Found a pharmacy about forty-five minutes away who sold two vials to a gentleman, and he paid for a hypodermic at the same time."

"Great job," she said. "But how'd you know this individual would be who we were looking for?"

He smiled. "Because I explained the situation and asked to see their security footage." He held up his cell phone and showed her the clip he took with his phone. "We'll have to subpoena the footage when it's time for court, but it's the same guy we've got sitting in the holding cell. That ties him to Mackie's murder, even if he refuses to talk."

When she frowned, that was the last reaction he expected.

"What's wrong Sheriff? I thought this would help to prove the case."

She nodded. "It does, and you did great work. But while you were out, the prisoner killed himself, so the evidence against him is useless."

The gleeful look he had on his face a moment ago deflated. But then he looked lost in thought and his eyes got bright again. "Well, we assumed he had an accomplice. There were two of them at the motel, right?"

This time, he looked at me for confirmation.

"Yes, but they were both wearing all black, so I wouldn't be able to identify them."

"Well, what if we have a vehicle that they might have been traveling in at the time?"

The sheriff and I looked at each other, surprised. This kid *was* on the ball.

"It would help a great deal," I said. "But how could you put the man in the pharmacy with the vehicle they were moving around in?"

His dimples showed when he smiled in response. "The Walmart in Springfield allows overnight parking, which means you never know who you're going to get," he said. "They have cameras all over the lot. So I also asked if I could see the footage during the time the man purchasing the insulin was inside the store. We know the murderers aren't local, so they had to have an out-of-state license plate, or a rental, which is what I was scrolling for. There were too many to count, so I got a little frustrated. But then, as I was viewing the footage, I spotted the guy walking out of the store. When he arrived at the parking spot, there was a moment where the driver appeared to be looking out the window. It was closed, and they were tinted, somewhat, but a savvy tech might get a facial recognition, or his ID might come up after you run the plate."

I was so ecstatic I kissed Deputy Boyd on the cheek. "You are going to make a fantastic detective someday."

"We don't have detectives here in Whispering Oak," he said.

"She's right, that was great work," the sheriff said, patting him on the back. "You went above and beyond. And if we had detectives, I can tell you'd be first rate."

His smile went wide from all the attention. "Do you want to run the plate?"

She pointed to him. "No, run it. Why should I get the glory when you did the work?"

I swear he almost skipped back to the office. We were still standing in the hall when he returned a few minutes later. He handed a sheet of paper to the sheriff. "License plate comes back to a Michaels Consulting Services, an LLC out of New York. The vehicle is described as a Ram Promaster conversion van, color is navy-blue."

"So it's like a camper that they could live out of while traveling, which means they wouldn't need a hotel?"

"Yep," he said. "I did a quick internet search. It has two sleeping areas, a dinette, a small kitchen, and a full bath with a shower."

"When they needed to empty their sewage, they could easily pull into a camping spot and pay a small fee to dump."

The sheriff glanced at me with her eyebrows raised. "You know a lot about camping?"

"I'm currently living in an RV after my home was torched."

"Your home was torched?"

"Long story," I said, and then smiled. "Unfortunately, you're not the only one who has had her life threatened."

"On that sad note, I should probably join the others with the ME at the holding cell," she said. "Do you have a place to stay after your motel room was turned into a crime scene? I doubt management has cleaned it up yet?"

I chuckled. "Since I expected they might show up, I paid for two rooms. One of them was still okay."

"Smart."

"Besides, I'm carrying, should he feel the need to return, it won't be two on one like it was before. The guy who rushed to my aid is also nearby, should I need help."

She nodded. "How about we regroup first thing in the morning? Oh, and by the way, an attorney for Mackie's sister called to see about collecting his body. When he asked, I informed him you had the original of his Will, and gave him your number to call. He said he would when they arrived in town. Guess she lives out of state."

Another thing to add to my regret list; that Mackie didn't get to say goodbye to any family members. "Whatever happened to Lucy?"

The sheriff smiled. "She's at my house with my husband and our other dog. Jerry's brother didn't want the dog and I couldn't see her going to the shelter."

"You're a softie at heart, aren't you?"

"Only with animals," she joked. "If you come up with anything you think I need to know before morning, just call."

"Will do," I said, and then I let myself out.

CHAPTER 28 - KATIE

OUTSIDE THE STATION, I sat in my SUV for a few moments and let the events over the last two days run through my mind. It was not that late, even though it was dark out. I took a quick drive over to the diner to get a comfort meal that Uncle Mackie always spoke so much about. I figured I'd bring my notepad and use it like I do a whiteboard writing out my thoughts, how things went down and the timeline, and what the possible endgame could be.

Along the way, I kept my eyes peeled for a blue Ram Promaster conversion van. It helped that I knew what vehicle to look for this time around. The men didn't accomplish what they set out to do when raiding my motel room, but would the one who wasn't captured stick around to make another attempt? Was the man in charge worried the one in custody would rat them out, or did he send the second man to enter the sheriff's station pretending to be an attorney to make sure he never talked again? From all I've learned, I knew Thomas Edwin Xavier was the man behind all of this, especially after Hal informed me he was the one who abused May. The Sheriff's response to his name only added more fuel. She had other fish to fry, or I would have questioned her further.

Did Xavier find out May was here in the U.S.? He's the only one whose involvement makes any sense, no matter how sadistic it is. So what is his goal? If he hoped to run for the highest office in the land, was he just trying to shut down any proof of his association with an abused woman who wound up living in America on the chance an opposite research firm learned of her existence? From all I've seen and heard regarding politics and the dirty tricks the parties play against each other, it wouldn't surprise me. Is winning the power of the presidency worth the death of three individuals to quash it?

I parked in the lot behind the diner, made sure the vehicle was locked and my backpack was with me before I walked inside. On the short walk from the lot to the door, I searched up and down the street and viewed every spot where a vehicle could hide. Thankfully, I didn't see any lurking vans.

The door rang from the bell when I entered. Like any small town, the locals glanced toward the entrance the minute there was a new arrival. The sign on the hostess desk said wait to be seated, so I took a moment to look around. I almost cried when I noticed framed images of my father, Rosie, and now Mackie, hanging on the back wall with messages from locals who heard about their passing.

The hostess walked toward me right then and noticed the tears that welled up in my eyes. "Are you okay?" she said, touching me gently on the arm.

I took a deep breath. "Yes, I just noticed the images on the back wall of two men that were very special to me."

"You knew Mackie and Donnie?" she said, with a surprised look on her face.

I nodded. "Donnie was my father; Mackie was his best friend."

She brought her hand to her chest, getting emotional herself. "Oh my, I am so sorry. We here at the diner loved those two men, and Rosie too,

Mackie's wife. It's going to be a lonely place here without them. There wasn't a day they were alive that one of them didn't show up with a smile, sharing tales that entertained the customers. Such a tragic ending for poor Mackie, but we don't know too much since the Sheriff is being tight-lipped. We just keep dropping off food to the deputies while they work tirelessly to help. We keep hoping they'll slip up and tell us what happened. Do you know?"

I shook my head. "Only what they allow me to know." I felt bad for holding out, but any local gossip could get into the hands of the wrong person and wind up as front-page news somewhere. We knew keeping it quiet wouldn't last, but we needed to control the timing.

She smiled. "Well, let me get you seated. Would you like Mackie's usual spot? I'm sure he would be honored."

"That would be nice. Thank you."

She seated me at the back table by the window. Like Mackie, I sat with my back against the wall so I had a view of the river, but I could also see who came inside.

"Here's a menu," she said. "If you need anything, holler. Your waitress will be here shortly. Again, I'm so sorry for your loss."

"Thank you," I said, sitting down and checking out the view, which wasn't much right now since it was dark. I bet it was awesome first thing in the morning when Mackie usually arrived.

I realized with all the lights on in the diner, I couldn't see much outside. But anyone passing by could clearly see me.

The waitress arrived with a glass of water, a napkin, and utensils. "Hi, my name is Tina and I'll be your server."

"Hi Tina," I responded. "I'm told you have some great comfort food here. What do you recommend?"

"That's easy," she said with a jovial smile. "The best comfort food is our homemade blackberry cobbler, but I guess you're referring to a meal first?" She winked.

"Food first, yes," I said, smiling in return.

"In that case, we have an awesome turkey plate with mashed potatoes and garlic, green bean casserole, a side of our homemade stuffing, and, of course, cranberry sauce and biscuits. Or you can try my favorite, which is the turkey pot pie. It's made with fresh turkey every day."

I smiled in return. "Turkey pot pie sounds great, and I'll take the cobbler for dessert, with maybe a scoop of vanilla ice cream."

"You got it," she said, writing it down on the pad in her hand. "You'll love both of them."

"I'm already salivating."

"I'll get that order in for you, then."

Once she left, I pulled out my notepad. First, I wrote out all the names of the players involved with whatever was going on. Underneath each name, I placed an arrow and then wrote abbreviated statements regarding their involvement or actions. No matter how many sentences were needed, I wrote them down.

Then I pulled out my cell phone and did an internet search for Thomas Edwin Xavier. The first link that popped up was a Wikipedia page, so I clicked on that and started reading. There was so much information listed from his early life, education, and military service. Whoever wrote and edited the page added years of incidents during his military career. He, too, was in Vietnam, but only during the last year before the war ended. During that time, he never met the three amigos. For the next three years of his military career, he traveled to various locations, Bosnia being his longest stay. After the four years, he did not re-enlist. Instead, he went private because of the financial benefits.

As far as I could tell, private military companies didn't become a thing until former Navy SEAL, Erik Prince founded *Blackwater*. Before that time, Tex teamed up with a few other former military members and they served as private security abroad for many years, until he founded his own firm: TSC, Inc., which stood for Tex Security Contractors, LLC, hence the nickname, I guess. That also explained why the three amigos didn't know him too well. They worked for separate PMC companies. Between the wealth of his family and the money his firm made, he became a multi-millionaire, quite young. After his first million, he also added an investment firm to his resume.

There were no negative comments about his investment firm on the page. The security company was flagged with quite a few lawsuits that were dismissed or settled out of court. In layman's terms, that meant they were never proven. Books were also written about some of those incidents where innocent individuals were allegedly killed, but Tex's firm was never named outright. Anyone could add or edit information on Wikipedia, so I knew to take what I read on the page with a grain of salt. But it made for pretty dark reading.

I wondered if all the stories I read or heard on the media about elections and opposition research firms were true. Could all the negative info be wiped clean from the internet if Thomas Xavier put his hat in the ring? During past elections, I heard media clips by some on the right that claimed *Google* and social media outlets were suppressing negative stories, but I didn't involve myself in politics too much to know if that was fact or fiction. Tex must have believed it was true, though. Otherwise, why go to all the trouble where May was concerned when all the negative allegations were floating around on the world-wide-web?

She's a real person with an actual story. If he found out she was in the U.S., he could have panicked because of the credible people she surrounded herself with. My father was a war hero, but he had already passed away. Hal and Mackie were also heroes. The three of them were warriors. And now Hal was a Senator with a solid reputation. If Tex got a hold of the photographs and kept May from talking, as a presidential candidate, he could then turn it around and use them against Hal. He could have him ousted or use them in some form of blackmail.

Of course, everything was just me thinking hypothetically, but that was the only way I could figure this shit out. The stuff on Wikipedia could be viewed as gossip that went nowhere. To the competition's opposition research firm, May might be viewed as a woman that could bring down his campaign. It would be like the political scandal years ago when the affair with Donna Rice was used to bring down presidential candidate Gary Hart. More recently, a similar tactic was used to keep a judicial nominee from being confirmed to the Supreme Court. The assertion was that the candidate sexually assaulted a woman years earlier when they were teenagers. There were no witnesses or any kind of proof to substantiate the story. In fact, during the hearing, the accuser's credibility was even called into question, and ultimately, the candidate was confirmed. But the nasty hearing and torment of the candidate's family left a stain on most of Americans.

I leaned back in the chair and shivered at the potential reality. If Tex really wants the power that comes with being president; how far would he go to stop others who want to keep it from happening?

The waitress arrived with my dinner, but she had a look of concern on her face. "You look a little stressed, dear. Is everything okay?"

"Oh yes, just some heavy reading, that's all."

"Well, here you go," she said with a smile. "This should help. Do you need more water or another drink?"

"No, I'm good, thanks," I said. "This looks great."

"You're going to love it."

I took a break from Wikipedia and devoured as much as I could. As good as it was; it still didn't equal Madison's homemade pot pie. That got me to thinking about my friends, Olivia and Madison. I hoped they were enjoying their cruise this time, since the last one was interrupted when they were kidnapped. When the cruise line heard about of the horror they suffered, they offered them a free cruise.

I took one more bite and knew I couldn't eat another. I moved it off to the side, appreciating that there was enough left over for a second meal. I could put it in the refrigerator at the motel and nuke it for dinner tomorrow if something didn't happen in the meantime. I put that out of my head and continued reading.

There was a link that said personal and family, so I clicked on it. I was surprised to read that Xavier was married to three different women over the last decade. The latest one divorced him three years ago. There were also a few sexual assault allegation suits, but each one was settled and NDAs signed, which meant I couldn't glean much information from them. I would have to do more search on that. I also knew that *some* lawsuits filed against individuals with money alleging sexual assault were found not to be credible. Sometimes, people with money are instant targets, but they can't be automatically discounted, either. I didn't know if that was the case with any of those lawsuits listed. But I had enough information about May's abuse to think they were true.

I wrote the names of his former wives, the date of marriage, and the date and reason for divorce. That data would be easy to track down, except for the one who lived in Dubai.

The waitress stopped by again. "How was it?"

"It was excellent, but so much food," I said. "Could you get me a to-go box, and do the same for the cobbler, and just forget the ice cream? I have to get back and finish up this reading."

"Sure thing," she said. "Let me get that for you." She grabbed the container of leftover pot pie and disappeared into the back.

I gathered up my notepad and stuffed it in my backpack, and pulled out my wallet. When she returned with the food in a bag, I handed her my credit card. While she went to ring me up, I noticed a van out the window. It was too dark to see the color, but the size fit with what I knew of a Ram conversion van. When she returned with the slip, I signed one copy and she handed me the other with my card.

"Thank you so much," she said. "I hope you come by to see us again."

"You can count it," I said, a little distracted by what I was seeing outside. I didn't know for sure if it was the van, but even if it was, I couldn't tell if it was close enough for the driver to see me. The van was parked by the river, with the front of the vehicle pointed this way. Was there enough light in the restaurant for him to have a clear view from that distance?

"Buck up, Katie," I said to myself as I slipped the backpack over my shoulders and got my keys ready. I waved to the waitress and hostess on the way out of the diner, and turned left to head back to my vehicle. I thought it better to avoid looking toward the van, but would do so once I was in the comfort of my own SUV. There was plenty of light in the lot, but I was protected from view by the building when I turned toward my vehicle. I remote-started it, unlocked it, and hopped into the driver's seat. Reversing out of the spot, I pulled the vehicle toward the street, and instead of turning left to head toward the motel, I turned right. As I continued on, the van was up on my left-hand side, and it was definitely the blue van. When I passed it, it took all my willpower to not turn my head and try to get a glimpse of the driver. But, as far as he knew, we weren't aware of the van.

Once I was a few blocks away, I realized he must not have seen me in the diner, but was just parked along the river for whatever reason. Maybe he just wanted to stay off the street while he planned his next attack. Either way, he didn't follow me, so I dialed dispatch at the sheriff's station. Gertrude was off duty, so I left a message with the deputy, advising him that the vehicle we were looking for was parked at the river. After I hung up, I wish I would have mentioned that they shouldn't show up with lights and sirens. Otherwise, a car chase might ensue in the small town, and the young deputy could be the one to get hurt. Nothing I could do to help, but I didn't want him to see me, so I took the side streets back to the motel.

CHAPTER 29 - KATIE

THERE WAS NO longer a reason for me to take precautions and drive around in circles to avoid a tail. One of the men involved just killed himself. The other already knew where I was. It didn't matter if he saw me pull into the motel parking lot. What mattered was me being ready for him if he showed up. I remembered that statement Sheriff Chase said that made me curious: she was more concerned about Thomas Edwin Xavier than a gang, because, as she said, you never knew he was going to send to come after you. But, thinking from a logical perspective, I didn't think Xavier wanted to bring too much attention to the situation. He wanted it contained to Whispering Oak. He may own a security contractor company, but I doubt that he'd send a team after me. They would definitely get noticed, especially in a small town. All it would take is one person to notify the news media.

If they were going to come after me to get the photographs and silence me, they'd do it in a one or two-man team. I already knew about the man in the blue van. I would have to stay alert for any newcomers. Even as a visitor to town, I already had a grasp of its residents. I noticed the guy in the Ford truck on the first day and wondered about his story. I knew absolutely nothing about him, but it was because of him that one of the bad guys was taken out of the equation. A new individual suddenly showing up would definitely stick out. Still, I couldn't help but wonder about the guy pretending to be an attorney visiting the prisoner. Was it the guy in the blue van?

I pulled into the spot in front of room eleven, shut off the engine, and placed the keys in the front pocket of the backpack. The Ford truck was in its usual spot in front of room nine. There was a yellow tape across the door to twelve that said: do not enter. The deputy and crime scene tech finished sweeping the room for evidence, so the manager was trying to keep people out.

I pulled the key card out of my pocket, slipped the backpack over my shoulder and grabbed the to-go box in my left hand so the right would be free if I needed to grab my gun. I checked the area one more time and then stepped out. As I walked toward the room, I glanced toward room nine. The dark curtains were open, revealing the sheers. The light was on inside and I could see the TV on as well. Impulsively, I walked toward the room and knocked.

When he answered the door, he looked suspicious, and I hesitated for a moment about what to say.

"Hi," I said, sheepishly. It wasn't often a woman knocked on a man's door at night that she didn't know. Plus, I wasn't sure of exactly what to say. I wanted to thank him for intervening, but also apologize that he was placed in harm's way. I'm sure when he rented a room at a small town motel where nothing ever happened, seeing two gunmen in the room next door was not something he expected. I also wanted to make sure he was okay. That knife wound seemed pretty wide.

"Hi," he responded, but he didn't look at all surprised to see me, but kept the door from opening too wide.

He was dressed in a pair of faded jeans, a white T-shirt, with bare feet. His face looked like he hadn't seen a razor in a few days. Maybe he was trying to grow a beard, or he just didn't bother to take the time. Before I interrupted, he was probably lying on the bed watching TV after taking one of the pain meds the hospital probably gave to him. I could tell his stomach was wrapped through the thin cotton of the shirt.

"I'm sorry to bother you, but I just wanted to make sure you're okay."

He shrugged like it was no big deal. "I'm alright. It would take more than a knife wound to keep me knocked down."

This was the first time I really spoke to him and noticed his accent. It sounded like he was from somewhere in the south. After what he did to help, the last thing I wanted to do was start questioning him about where he was from, making him feel more like a perp. Besides, I was sure the sheriff already got that information.

"I also wanted to thank you," I said. "I appreciate you putting yourself in potential danger for someone you don't know. Because of you, one of them was arrested."

"I didn't realize there were two of them when I first went in," he said. "That wouldn't have stopped me, but I might have entered with a different approach had I known?"

"I'm sorry you even had to."

He looked away, his eyes filled with uncertainty. "To be honest, when I entered, I assumed you were in the room."

I gulped, feeling even more guilt. He came in trying to save me, only I escaped from the room once I heard them enter room eleven. It was my fault he was injured.

"I'm so sorry," I said, well, because what else could I say?

"Who were those guys, anyway?"

If he was just a local, I would probably give him a half-truth, fearing the gossip. Since he got injured trying to help me, lying just didn't seem right. Besides, if he was in the military, he knew they had some skills, too.

I paused for a moment before answering, making sure that my words were vague, without lying outright. "They were looking for something in my possession they think could get their boss in trouble,"

"Who is their boss?"

Now it felt like I was the one on the hot seat. "He's somebody with a lot of money who also wants the power."

He smirked. "That means you can't tell me. He sounds like a politician."

"Something like that," I said. I could tell from the look in his eyes that he knew what the subtle statement meant.

His cell phone rang, and he backed away from the door to look at the screen. I got the sense he needed to answer it. "I'll let you go. You probably need to get that. I just wanted to thank you. Have a good night."

When I moved away from the door, I glimpsed the pair of cowboy boots on the floor next to the bed. The sight of them made my pulse quicken, and I sped up getting to my room, two doors down. My hands were suddenly shaking as I put the key card into the lock. When the green light blinked, I hurried inside, shut the door behind me, and made sure it was locked. A wave of weariness hit me and I dropped to the floor on my knees.

Get a grip, Katie. Millions of people wear cowboy boots, I told myself. You included. His accent was from the south, cowboy boots were common there. They just weren't in Massachusetts. That's why the sight of them struck me so fast. And that the guy pretending to be an attorney—who so brazenly waltzed into the sheriff's station—was wearing them too. I tried to remember the security footage Sheriff Chase played, showing the man in the suit, cowboy hat, and boots. What color were they? They were black, to match the cowboy hat. The boots at the end of his bed were black, too.

Still, I own a pair of black boots. My ex-husband had black boots. That could mean nothing. It could also mean something. The only thing I knew for sure was that I'd be sleeping with my gun next to my pillow tonight. If I could get any sleep at all.

The unexpected sound of three light taps on the door caused me to stand up and grip my gun. Could it be? I moved toward the door and peered out of the peephole.

Breathing a sigh of relief, I opened the door and stayed behind the door to allow Finn to enter.

"Hi babe," he said, though he immediately registered my angst and walked through the door without question and dropped a duffel bag he was carrying on the floor by the chair.

Once he was inside, I shut the door with my boot, dropped my backpack, removed my gun belt and placed it on the desk before I fell into his arms.

"Oh Finn," I said, as the tears for Mackie filled my eyes. And then I unloaded everything that happened. How I was worried about Hal, a woman that I didn't know, and her daughter, Sierra. And that something my father and his two friends did all those years ago was now bringing danger to this small town and the sheriff and her young deputies. After I unburdened myself and dumped everything onto this poor man's shoulders, he took my face into his hands and kissed me on the lips.

"Well, what do you think I came here for?" The gleam in his eyes was followed by his teasing smile.

I didn't know what it was about this man; he always seemed to show up at the right time, and knew just what to say and do, to snap me out of my funk. He comforted me without even trying.

"By that look in your eyes, I'd say you came here for something other than helping me with my investigation," I teased as I nuzzled his neck. "Besides, I thought you were working on a case of your own."

"That I am," he said, lacing his fingers through my hair, which sent a tingle down my spine. "I have a partner. He's got eyes on the mark. You've got me until morning. If something goes down, or things ratchet up, he'll send me a 911. I can be there in less than a half-hour."

I narrowed my eyes. "You've been this close?"

"We're still at the recon stage; who knows where the op will take us, but yeah, right now we're not too far," he said. "I'm here to assist. So use me however you need to."

And there was that wicked grin again.

"Oh, what the hell," I said. I pulled off his leather jacket and then unbuttoned his shirt. "Let's get this sexual tension out of the way first, and then we can deal with this fiasco of a case after we're done."

"You will not hear me say no," he said.

The next thing I knew, we were helping each other remove the other's clothing and boots. In just a few minutes, we were undressed, kissing each other and exploring each other's bodies as if it was the last chance we'd get. And for a little more than an hour, I could put the fear I had for Hal, May, and Sierra to the back of my mind.

CHAPTER 30 - KATIE

IT WAS DARK outside, but I knew it was already morning when I woke up, because my phone kept pinging, to notify me I had emails. I felt around for Finn, but his side of the bed was empty. For a second, I thought he must have gotten the 911 call telling him he had to go, so I looked on my phone for a text—like the last time. But then I heard the shower turn on. I smiled and jumped out of bed. Desire flooded through me as I hurried into the bathroom.

"If I only have you for a couple more hours, I might as well make it worthwhile," I teased as I stepped into the shower and rubbed my hands along his back.

Giving me that devil may care smile I knew so well, he turned around and pulled me to his chest. "You're insatiable, you know that?"

"Only with you," I said, and I actually meant it. I was married for over two decades, but couldn't remember ever craving my ex the way I desired Finn. Maybe that's why things fell apart the way they did and my life was almost destroyed. Instead of trying to fix what was broken, my ex lived a double life and played out his dark fantasies with psycho women, but wanted to keep me as the loving wife tending to the home. For a moment, I realized how much it still hurt to think about. I shook off the depressing thoughts of the past and focused on the man in front of her. When I tilted my head up and looked into his eyes, I saw the same hunger in them that stirred the lust in various parts of my body.

"Let's make sure that doesn't change," he teased. He traced his fingers along my cheek before he lowered his lips to mine.

When he slipped his tongue into my mouth, it stirred the passion in both of us. We wrapped our arms around each other until we both lost control.

"This just feels so right," he said, and for another hour, I forgot all the madness going on around us and we just enjoyed each other.

***

Wearing Finn's shirt, I straddled the wooden chair and took turns feeding both of us bites of the blackberry cobbler. He was standing in front of a whiteboard he brought with him, reviewing the notes I made at the diner the night before.

A manila folder was opened on the edge of the bed with more reading material that Derek provided. Most of it was a lengthy background on Thomas Edwin Xavier, verifying and adding to what I already picked up off of the Wikipedia page. The documents showed where he lived and spent most of his time in Lloyd Harbor, New York. I knew where his main office was located, that he owned thousands of acres in upper state New York where he built his training camp for the security firm, and a second office in Abu Dhabi. The file also detailed the info on his summer home in the Hamptons, and the penthouse apartment on 5th Avenue in New York City, though he rarely spent any time there.

"In some respects, he's like the New York version of Derek on paper," I said, reading through the profile Derek provided.

He shook his head from side to side. "No comparison. The two men are filthy rich, founded security firms and invest in real estate; but that's where their similarities end. Derek had one wife who was taken away from him when she was kidnapped and murdered," Finn said, not even bothering to hide his disdain for the man I was investigating.

"Thomas Edwin Xavier aka Tex is a womanizing dick who abused at least one woman that we know of. But we suspect there are dozens more, only the victims can't talk because of NDAs they were forced to sign. I'm convinced he's behind what's going on, just as much as you are."

"Sheriff Chase is former NYPD," I said. "She said his involvement just made the case more convoluted."

"It became convoluted decades ago," he said. "Where do you want to start?"

I studied the information he had written on the whiteboard to help me with my next step. "I promised Sierra that I'd find out the truth about what happened to her mother. I am afraid to do anything else until I know that. Did Xavier kidnap her? Is she dead?"

He rubbed the back of his neck. "If he had a history of abusing her before she ran away, and found her, while trying to get his hands on all the photographs that prove he knew her—"

"I know," I said in a shaky voice. "The prospect of her being alive is not good."

He walked up to me, placed his fingers under my chin, and tilted it until my eyes reached his. "You should prepare yourself for that possibility," he said, and then kissed me lightly on the lips.

I took a breath. "I don't want to think, but let's say she is dead," I said, calling on my inner strength. "What are the odds there were CCTV cameras in the area that she went walking the morning she left and never returned?"

"Framingham is a fairly large city with headquarters for some of the biggest companies in Massachusetts. I'd say it's highly likely. But I doubt they'd have somebody monitoring them."

"So there could be footage of May walking in the area before she disappeared?"

He shrugged. "You won't know unless you ask. Text the street names to Derek. With his connections, you know he won't need a warrant to get the footage."

"Poor Derek, I'm inundating him with work for Connie and Roger these days." But I did as he suggested, sent Derek a text with the route May normally walked to see if he could find any footage, and followed it with: this is a 911 emergency. I wasn't naïve enough to believe Derek would find a video that showed someone abducting May in broad daylight, but Sierra said that's when she disappeared. Maybe somebody in the neighborhood was walking in the area at the same time. It needed to be checked. The one thing I've learned since becoming a PI; you could spend days or weeks turning over every rock looking for answers and when you're just about to give up, it could be under that next rock that you find it.

Finn studied me for a moment. "Katie, I see that determined look in your eyes. I've seen it a few times over the last few months when you were working on your cases. As sure as I'm standing her, I know you're going after this guy, Xavier, Tex, or whatever name he goes by."

"I have to," I said, and stopped talking the minute he put up his hand to let me know he wasn't finished.

"What I'm trying to say is; you're going to have to play it smart. You can't just go in guns blazing with a guy like him. He has a security firm that could shoot you before you enter his front door. You need to study everything you can about him to see what makes him tick, what his weak points are."

I stared at him, while digesting what he was trying to tell me without coming right out and saying it. "You mean like I did with my stalker?"

My stalker was Derek's stepdaughter who had histrionic personality disorder, among many other terrifying traits. One of her main delusions was the belief that she could have and take anything she wanted, and she wanted my husband. Her one weakness was the belief that she was adored by everyone, and she turned into a raging lunatic when she learned she wasn't. I used that aspect to my advantage.

"Exactly like you did to your stalker," he said. "You know what this guy Xavier is afraid of, so use it against him."

"The tabloid media."

He lifted his shoulders as if to shrug, but his sardonic smile let me know I was on the right track.

CHAPTER 31 - KATIE

AFTER FINN LEFT to go deal with his own case, I got dressed and gathered up all the documents and placed them in my backpack. Once I secured the gun belt to my hip and shrugged on my bomber jacket, I sprinkled more baby powder by the door. I took one last look around to make sure I didn't forget anything, and then grabbed the whiteboard and left the room.

When I was outside, I stood by the door for a moment and looked around. The Ford truck was gone, and there were still no other guests. I never got around to asking him how long he was staying at the motel, so I didn't know if he was out getting coffee or breakfast, or if he checked out. Looking toward the office, the light was still off, which meant the manager was still in the back. I assumed there was a small apartment back there, where she stayed.

I strode toward my SUV, opened the back, and stored the whiteboard inside. When I got behind the wheel, I thought about Finn's advice and the more I analyzed the idea, the more I thought it might work. But before I put anything in motion, I needed to check with Derek on the CCTV footage in Framingham and stop by the sheriff's office. I wanted to see if her deputy had any luck with the blue van.

First, I took a quick drive a few miles down the road, which actually took me into the next town and entered a local grocery mart. After walking the aisles for something that looked appetizing, I settled on some zero sugar iced tea with caffeine, peanut butter crackers, and a couple of apples the clerk told me were delivered from the farmer's market that morning. Back in the car, I took a long drink of the iced tea, hoping the caffeine would help to rejuvenate me, and stayed there while I devoured an apple. After another gulp of the tea, I headed back toward town.

"Good morning, Katie," Gertrude said in her usual pleasant voice.

"Good morning, Gertrude. What's all this?" I asked, though I suspected I already knew. The counter just above the dispatch desk was covered with fruit, donuts, and pastries.

"Isn't it wonderful?" she said. "Our friends at the diner dropped them off first thing this morning for the sheriff and deputies working tirelessly on the recent murders.

"That is so nice of them."

She nodded. "We have some of the best people living in this quaint town. You can go on back. The sheriff was running around trying to get things done, but I think she might be in her office by now."

"Thanks, Gertrude."

I headed through the door and down the hall. When I reached the sheriff's office, her desk was empty, so I went inside to wait. I just sat down and was about to slip off my backpack when she rushed in, looking frazzled, and grabbed a phone off her desk.

"Oh hey, Katie," she said. "I was just about to call you. You'll want to follow me in your car. We found the blue van."

I stood back up. "I know. Last night, I called in the location."

She shook her head and stormed back out of the office with me following. "Oh no, the deputy had no luck last night. The van wasn't where you said it was when he arrived. We just got the call."

I raised my eyebrows. "Just now? Where is it?"

"It's parked a couple of blocks away from the motel."

That thought made me shiver.

"An elderly woman who lives in the area said she saw the van parked on the street last night," the sheriff continued. "She saw the driver get out and go for a walk, but he returned not long after. She thought he was just visiting someone, so she went to bed. A short time ago, she heard a noise that woke her up. She looked out the window and saw it was still there, so she called us."

"Where's the driver?"

She frowned. "You'll see."

I followed her out, and we both stepped into our respective SUVs. When I saw her switch on the lights and siren, I realized we weren't just going to look at an empty van.

Deputy Boyd was already on the scene when we arrived. She parked her vehicle next to his, and I parked in a spot across the street. I could see the blood on the driver's side window and suspected what had happened before I even left the vehicle. When we stepped and walked over, she placed her hand up to keep me from getting too close, so all I could see was the view from the windshield. The man's head was slumped downward and to the side, toward the window.

She walked toward the passenger door of the Ram van, slipped her hands into a pair of latex gloves, and studied the scene.

"Bastard shot himself," she said to her deputy, but I was close enough to hear.

"Are you sure he didn't get a visit from the guy pretending to be an attorney?"

She glanced at me. "How do we know he wasn't the one pretending to be the attorney?" the sheriff countered. "I'll need confirmation, but it looks like he shot himself on the right side of the head."

She brought her right hand up, and showed me a demonstration of how it could have been done, as if she was holding a gun and aiming it at her head.

"The blood sprayed on the driver's side window. The gun is still in his hand, but positioned in such a way that looks like it was involuntary when it landed."

"You mean it doesn't appear as though a killer staged the scene?"

"Again, I'll need to get it confirmed, but that's the way it appears."

While she and Deputy Boyd did their thing, I walked back toward my vehicle to stay out of the way. If he was planning to kill himself, even though it wasn't confirmed yet, why did he park so close to the motel? And where did he go when the elderly woman said he took a walk? I ran a bunch of scenarios through my head when a thought occurred to me. I walked back toward the van.

"Hey Sheriff, I'm going to run back to the motel," I yelled, and waited until she waved back, letting me know she got the message.

When I pulled into the lot, the lights were on in the office and I could see the manager at the desk. The Ford truck was still gone, and the door to room twelve was open and a maid was inside cleaning. When I parked in my spot and stepped out, I noticed a note on the door to room eleven: please stop by the office.

Frowning, I headed that way and wondered if she planned to ask me to leave after what happened. She was on the phone when I entered the office door, but handed me a small package.

"This was dropped inside the overnight mail slot on the door last night," she said, holding a hand over the phone.

"Can I ask by whom?"

She shrugged. "I assumed he was a delivery person."

There were only a few people who knew I was at the motel besides Olivia, Madison, Derek and Finn; those at the sheriff's office, and the bad guys. Did one of them drop this off before he killed himself?

"Okay, thanks," I said, hurrying back to my room.

Once I was inside, I checked the white powder. No footprints, but then again, both bad guys that I knew about were now dead. The only one remaining that was in question was the alleged attorney. I sat down on the edge of the bed and opened the envelope. A cell phone was inside.

CHAPTER 32 - KATIE

MY HANDS STARTED shaking. I didn't know what I had. Was I going to see something horrific? I took a deep breath and tried to calm my nerves. I pushed the button on the side to turn the phone on. I was surprised to see that it wasn't password protected. It went right to the home screen. It looked like somebody went through and deleted apps and anything that could give me the identity of the user. There were only two icons: the one for phone calls and the gallery icon.

I clicked on the phone icon. There were no incoming calls. But there were several calls made, but they all went to the same number. There was nothing on the phone to show who owned the phone or who belonged to that number. But I had a suspicion when I realized it was a New York area code.

I exited out of that and clicked on the gallery. There were several videos. Each one had a date above it, but no label or title to describe what it was. I got the sudden feeling of déjà vu when I noticed one video was dated on the day of the break-in at Mackie's house and the neighbor was killed.

Hesitating for a moment, I forced myself to click the video. A man's face appeared on the screen. He was taking part in a face-time call with the recipient. It took me a minute of listening before I realized that what I was seeing and listening to was Thomas Edwin Xavier's face and voice, after the break-in and murder of Mackie's neighbor. He and the two men he hired, whose voices were also recorded—though their faces weren't shown—were discussing what to do next.

I exited out of that one and clicked on the next video and listened to it for several minutes. It was the same players.

Seeing Thomas Edwin Xavier on the screen, I realized he was younger than each of the three amigos. Each one of them had a distinguished look about them. Xavier was rougher around the edges. I suppose some would consider him attractive, especially those that appreciated his wealth. But he spent too much time in the sun, which intensified the lines around his eyes and mouth. Maybe he was a smoker, or possibly into cigars, which was more likely for a multi-millionaire.

When I completed listening to the few videos in order, I learned quite a few things. It confirmed the two men who came after me were former military; I suspected they had some skills. The one who was jailed was Stefan. I also understood why the man in the van may have killed himself. From what I gathered, he didn't take part in the actual killing. He knew they were going to break into Mackie's home and steal the photos, but it didn't sound like he was on board for killing the innocent neighbor.

They also talked about killing me and Mackie. It chilled me to the bone that they had so much background on me and knew about my personal life. I remember Derek warning me that someone was looking into my background.

The section in one video that had me on the edge of my seat was when Xavier talked about blackmailing Hal. He also said they didn't have to worry about the woman in the photographs because she was being handled. When the men questioned him, he said: she's in my possession.

He was hiding her somewhere?

I leaned back on the bed to think. "I've got the frigging payload! But what was the best way to deal with it and get May back alive?"

CHAPTER 33 - KATIE

I PULLED MYSELF to an upright position on the end of the bed. I grabbed my cell phone and punched in Derek's number. It rang several times before he finally picked up.

"What's wrong Katie," he said, his voice filled with concern.

"Has Finn filled you in on everything up to now?" I said, rubbing my temples to keep a headache at bay. Finn and Derek seemed to communicate more than I was aware of, but it warmed my heart to know that they were both watching over me.

"Our last conversation was getting the update about the prisoner taking himself out with cyanide. Then I received your text regarding the footage in Framingham. Connie is working on that."

"I'm in over my head, Derek."

"Talk to me."

"I believe Thomas Edwin Xavier has May in his possession. I currently have videos where he is face-timing with the two men he hired to do the break-in at Mackie's, and the murder."

"How the hell did you get your hands on those?"

"One man he hired had a conscience," I said. On one hand, I was elated that I had the proof. I was also terrified they would try to take it away.

"He left them for me at the front desk of the motel. He killed himself after. The sheriff found his body in the van they were traveling in a little over an hour ago."

"Do the videos have enough to point directly at Thomas Xavier?"

"Yes. They talked about all of it. How he wanted me and Mackie taken out of the equation. They also talked about blackmailing Hal once they got their hands on the images. When Xavier had the situation contained, he was going to announce his run. He could then use the truth about Hal's involvement to coerce him for an endorsement and any other issues that suited him."

Derek was quiet for a moment. "Do you think Xavier knows his man is dead yet?"

I shrugged, even though Derek couldn't see me. "I don't see how. The Sheriff has been good about keeping the media at bay."

But who was the man who was brazen enough to walk into the sheriff's station claiming to be an attorney?

"So, what's your greatest concern right now?" Derek said.

"Two things: I'm concerned about the safety of the evidence in my possession."

"I can clone the phone, Katie."

"I hadn't considered that, but that will make me feel better knowing there's a copy. I also need to figure out how to use it to get May back?"

Again, he was quiet while I assumed he was analyzing the data, most of which he had from doing all the background searches. "If you're asking for my advice, I suggest you find his weakness and hit him head on."

I laughed sarcastically. He was saying almost verbatim what Finn suggested I do. "Thomas Edwin Xavier isn't Lexy," I said, knowing he was advising me to use the same techniques I used on his stepdaughter.

"If you do a little more reading up on Thomas Edwin Xavier, I think you'll find that his and Lexy's narcissistic and manipulative personalities are quite similar. Neither one of them wanted the public to know their true nature, which is why they did everything in the shadows. The only difference is; he has the millions to hire others to do his dirty work. But trust me; this man cares about the media scrutiny. Otherwise, he could have hired an entire team to descend into the small town of Whispering Oak. I bet when all is said and done, you'll learn that the men he hired didn't have reputable backgrounds either."

"I already know, but how did you? In the videos he mentioned that the two he hired were dishonorably discharged."

Derek grunted. "I've known enough military men in my days. A reputable former military man would not break into the home of a Veteran who honorably served—with the medals to prove it—and would willingly do him harm, just to save the ass of an egotistical man with delusions of grandeur who thinks he can be president, no matter how much money was in play."

"I don't know what those men did that got them dishonorably discharged, but I believe one of them was trying to make things right, or as right as they could be after what they'd done, which is why he gave me his phone."

"That might be, but he did so you could bring the man down. Trust me, Katie, you can handle Xavier. You're a lot stronger and smarter than you think."

"It sounds like you and Finn are both suggesting I go at Xavier using the media arsenal, but have a back-up plan, if necessary?"

"Like I said, read the full report Connie put together on Xavier, not just his business background. And then talk to the sheriff. I bet the two of you can put together the right scheme to deal with him."

After we disconnected, I did as Derek suggested and read through the entire report on Thomas Edwin Xavier. He was right. I saw him in a whole new light. The report gave a more in-depth view into his brief marriages, but also the lawsuits that were filed against him by women he dated. Those suits were ultimately settled, checks paid to the victims, but they were also sealed after Xavier alleged his job was a matter of national security, because of the high profile of some of his clients. Since the women didn't oppose the motion, the court caved. If any journalist went in search of the details on each case, they would be out of luck.

Since I couldn't read the actual lawsuits, I did an internet search for media headlines during the dates in question. What I gleaned from articles put out by the tabloids—which he tried to sue to quash the stories—was that he had a penchant for bondage, that he dismissed the women when they said no, and then took things too far. Yep, there were definitely similarities. Take away his millions and he was Lexy in a pantsuit.

I did a few more searches of his name directly on the sites of various tabloids over the years. Once I knew what this man was all about, I formed a plan. I was pretty sure Sheriff Chase would be happy to assist if I could convince her that this route was the best way to handle it. I didn't know if we could get the outcome we preferred, but if I could help Sierra find her mother, that would be a start.

For the first time since Finn had me smiling in the shower that morning, I felt self-assured once again and fully confident I could handle the likes of Thomas Edwin Xavier.

CHAPTER 34 - KATIE

SHERIFF CHASE STARED at me as if I'd lost my mind. "Do you need a reminder? You only agreed to share certain evidence with me, because you were certain I would agree with you and keep it from the media? And now you want to go to the media?"

"I know, Sheriff," I said, feeling like I was being scrutinized, just like her deputies must have felt under her powerful gaze.

"At the time, I was concerned about them learning of Hal's involvement, and feared May would be deported after it was revealed she was smuggled into the country. And then there was her daughter to think about. As of this moment, Xavier doesn't know she exists."

Before her questioning me, I spent the last two hours showing her all the background on Thomas Edwin Xavier that Derek provided; some she already knew or heard from her former job with the NYPD. After she finished reading, she shook her head.

"Convoluted," I reminded her.

"Convoluted," she agreed.

Then, I let her view the videos on the cell phone, and informed her of how I came to have them in my possession. The minute she heard him call her a small-town sheriff, she was ready to take a ride to New York, but I reminded her he had May in his possession and we had to have a plan first.

"If you go to the media, you know everything will come out," she argued.

I shook my head. "Not if I can control the narrative."

She frowned. "No disrespect, but I've never known the media to be controlled? But better yet, how would you go about it, if they could?"

"The media can be controlled if we offer something that is beneficial to them. Look at how they were controlled by certain political parties during elections. Opposition research teams use them all the time to put out a message they want to manipulate the public into believing. That's what I'll be doing. I will hand-feed material to a select reporter I know at The Gossip Zone, TGZ. It's a tabloid magazine in New England, but their celebrity and political reach is wide. I've dealt with her before. Her headlines get clicks. She'll give it just enough juice to get Xavier worried. Then she'll put it all over social media. Hungry journalists will pick it up and park outside each of his properties, which will make him lose control."

"That sounds like a dangerous game."

"Dangerous, but necessary," I said. "Once he contacts the reporter and threatens to sue, that's when I call him. I will demand that he release May into my custody, or I will start releasing videos that show him hiring two men, and conspiring to assassinate Mackie and myself, and planning to extort a United States Senator. He'll likely demand a trade, which means he'll only give me May if I give him the phone. He'll also threaten to ruin Hal, and have May deported, but I don't think it will come to that. This will keep him from ever running for office, but hopefully, reunite a mother and daughter."

"I must have missed something in that scenario. How do you placate the reporter?"

"That's where you come in," I said, smiling, but inside my gut was going crazy with worry. "After we have May away from that lunatic, you'll have all the evidence, so you can do what you need to do to bring the bastard down. The reporter will be happy, because she will get the front-page news headline before any other outlet. That's all they care about is getting it first."

I could tell by her reaction that she was awed by the audaciousness of the plan, but she still had doubts. "How will you give me the video evidence if you have to hand the phone over to Xavier for the exchange?"

"Derek's people are going to make a clone. Xavier won't get the original, but he won't be able to tell the difference."

She leaned back and stared at me, then smiled.

"So, are you on board?"

"Does this mean a trip to New York to make this happen?"

I shrugged. "I'm not sure. Studying all the real estate he owns, I would think his Lloyd Harbor property is where he's keeping May. According to the doorman, he has a tenant in the 5th Avenue property. His house in the Hamptons doesn't offer much privacy. He wouldn't take her to the training facility where his employees train."

She unexpectedly chuckled.

"What so funny?"

"I just think it's ironic that this whole sordid mess started because he abused a woman… hopefully, it's going to be another woman who brings him down."

I gave her a reassuring smile. "I have full faith in you to do just that."

***

"You're doing this now?" Sheriff Chase said with a look of surprise on her face as she came around the desk to view what I was laying out a short time later.

"Who knows what May is going through in his care?" I said.

"Enough said."

She stood behind me and looked over my shoulder. I had the report of Thomas Xavier to the left of me, and photographs from old tabloid headlines in front of me. They showed images of Xavier with several women in various bondage poses. Some were women who ultimately sued him. In these, their faces were blackened out. I typed out a few different headline options the reporter could use, along with narratives to coincide with the story.

"The reporter's goal is to infer the story is about a potential presidential candidate, but keep the language vague to avoid the viability of a lawsuit," I said. "She might post some of the old images and ask: is it the same man? My goal is to piss him off, but also alert him to the possibility of becoming major headline news, which would quash any presidential run."

"You're one sneaky dame," she said.

I slipped everything into a manila envelope, and then called for a messenger to deliver them immediately. The reporter would then look over my ideas, but put her own slant on the headlines, articles, or footage she uses.

"When do you plan on making this happen?"

"Her final copy should hit the internet later today, which would be picked up by other hungry reporters and civilian journalists on the web, and then mainstream media will inevitably show snippets during their nightly news. By the nine o'clock hour, most of them will have their talking heads speculating about his future."

"I hope you know what you're doing," she said, giving me a questioning look. "It feels like you've done this before."

I nodded. "A woman wasn't being held captive in the other situation, but I have. The PR campaign did what it was intended, but I still suffered a setback because of it."

"What happened?"

"The target went down, but she manipulated a disturbed woman into torching my cottage."

The sheriff's mouth dropped open in surprise. "So that's how you lost your home... but you know this could end with you losing more than a material possession?"

I sighed. "You heard the videos. He already wants to kill me."

"This could make the threat worse."

"Tell me something Sheriff; if you weren't concerned about the safety of your husband, would you have given up the NYPD after your life was threatened for helping a teenager? Or would you still be in New York taking down gang members, one thug at a time?"

She hesitated. "I see your point."

"Let me leave you with this," I added, feeling bolder now that I could see an end to this game, along with the reminder of what Derek said. "Thomas Edwin Xavier, aka Tex, is a multi-millionaire who founded a security company. He no longer runs the day-to-day operations of the company, but he has access to all the personnel who are said to be former military or law enforcement individuals. With all those highly skilled Veterans, why would he only hire two sad sacks that were dishonorably discharged and probably didn't even work for the security firm?"

I could see her working it out in her mind, but at first she didn't get the point. "But that report shows various allegations of questionable incidents over the years."

I nodded. "Notice how most of those allegations were overseas, money paid, and what really happened hushed up?"

Her eyes furrowed. "Okay, I'll give you that one, but what are you suggesting without coming right out and saying it?"

I smiled. "If you're like me, you glossed over most of the report and didn't pay attention to things that occurred years ago. I was focused on his abuse of women. Notice how he stepped down as the CEO of the security firm and somebody new took over. He's still listed as the Chairman, but he no longer has any dealings with the operations. Here in the U.S. he wants the security firm to be well-respected, which starts at the top."

"I get it," she said. "He doesn't want the reputable former military or police officers who work for his security firm to know who he really is."

My look said it all. She hit the nail on the head. That's what Derek and Finn were trying to make me see; that Xavier and the woman who stalked me were so similar. Like Lexy, Xavier had two personas. The one he presented to the public was an intelligent and well-respected businessman who founded a security company and turned it into a multi-million-dollar venture. Yet, in private, his addiction toward sexual bondage became his weapon of choice against the women who were unfortunate enough to engage with him.

"Just please be careful," she said. "We still don't know who the man was that came in claiming to be an attorney. He could be another man with a questionable background. And to be blunt; you're putting yourself out there as bait."

CHAPTER 35 - KATIE

I RETURNED TO the motel to go through all the evidence and notes one more time to see if there were any cracks in my plan. The manager was at her desk, probably reading one of her mystery books. She didn't look up when I drove by. The Ford truck was still gone. I wondered if he had checked out. I never got his story. Not that he felt like sharing.

I knew things were coming down to the wire when two things happened. I received a text from my contact at The Gossip Zone tabloid magazine telling me the headline article regarding Xavier would go live at the six o'clock hour. Social media posts would follow on *Twitter, Facebook, Instagram,* and *TikTok.* The minute that happened, the shit would hit the fan with journalists pushing for answers.

Then I received an email notification from Derek telling me they tracked down the CCTV footage where May went walking in Framingham on the day she disappeared.

I clicked on the link for the video and pushed play. It looked like a street in a suburban neighborhood. The houses were single family ranch homes on both sides of the street. The landscaping was kept up to date. Trash cans and recyclable bins were at the end of each driveway with the lids off, which meant the garbage and recycle trucks already emptied them. So far, I didn't see any individuals.

I glanced toward the lower right-hand corner. There was a time stamp that said 9:45 a.m. Seconds later, a dark-haired woman came into view. She was dressed in a black Adidas athletic suit with white stripes and lettering and white tennis shoes. I knew it was Adidas, because I owned the same suit. She remained in the camera's sight as she walked along the sidewalk, and then the video went blank. Seconds later, the video continued. Only now, the woman was on a different street. Two other women were walking on the other side of the street. The time in the corner said 10:26. By then, she had been walking for forty-one minutes. I realized what I was viewing were separate videos that Derek's IT tech, Connie, sliced together.

Once it paused and started again, the time was then 10:45. She had been walking for an hour. But this time, there was a vehicle on the street behind her. I could only see the front of the vehicle. It was black. Not enough of a view to tell make or model. The next time the video paused, I assumed it would be gone, and that it was just a local in the area. But when the video started again, I saw the vehicle all the way to the back window. It was a black Ford truck with a flag and army sticker on the back window. The woman was being followed by the same truck that had been parked in front of room nine the last couple of days.

I quickly dialed the burner phone I gave to Sierra. "Hi Sierra, do you remember what your mother was wearing the day she went walking and disappeared?"

"A black jogging suit," she said, suddenly wary. "Why? Did you find her?"

"I haven't found her, but I'm looking," I said, trying to keep my promise. "Try not to worry, too much."

"Please, find her," she said. "She's all I have."

237

"I'm doing everything I can."

"Dammit!" I said to myself when I hung up.

I let the video play out to see if it showed the actual abduction. It did not. The camera lost view of her when she ran down a side street, which was camera-free, or he nabbed her in a blind spot. Running the scenario through my mind; the guy in the truck must have abducted, subdued her, and then transported her to New York. The truck was already parked at the motel when I arrived and got a room, but according to Sierra, her mother had been gone almost a week by then. He had plenty of time to get to and from New York. Seeing the black boots and adding it in with this video, I'd bet on it he was the one impersonating an attorney to get into the holding cell.

Normally, I keep it to myself that I am a private investigator. But I was about to make an exception. Being such a small town, I was pretty sure the manager had heard the rumors about the deaths of two locals by now. She hadn't mentioned them, but if the diner knew, most of the townspeople heard. I could picture the locals sitting down to breakfast at the diner and the gossip jumping from one table to the next. I slipped my backpack over my shoulder, put the key card in my pocket, and locked the door on the way out.

When I entered the office, the manager looked up, put a bookmark to save her spot in the book, and walked up to the counter.

"Hi, what can I help you with today?"

"You know, I don't think I ever got your name," I said, noticing she never wore a nametag.

"It's Mitzi," she said.

"I'm sure you already heard the stories about the two locals dying, and of course, what happened here?"

She nodded, but suddenly looked apprehensive, probably wondering how it involved her.

I slipped my hand in the backpack and reached for my wallet, flipping it open as I pulled it up to show her. "I wasn't just here to meet with a friend. I was here investigating a crime. One of those locals who died was my father's best friend."

"I'm so sorry," she said, sounding genuinely concerned. "Is there anything I can do?"

"Actually, I was hoping you could tell me a little about the guest staying in room nine," I said.

Her eyes got huge. "Is he involved somehow?"

I nodded, sheepishly. "He could be. Did he say where he was from?" I was kicking myself for not even noticing his license plate. I was paying attention to the stickers on the back window.

Her forehead creased. "I'm not sure I feel comfortable telling you that. Did he do something wrong? The other night, he got stabbed helping you. Why didn't you ask him then?"

"I should have," I admitted. "But because he helped me, I wasn't suspicious. But now—"

"Now, you are suspicious?"

"I am suspicious."

She nibbled on her lip. I knew she was torn between wanting to help and protecting the privacy of her clientele.

"If you can't tell me where he's from, could you at least have the maid go into his room and tell me if she sees certain items? If I tell you what they are?"

She frowned. "That seems even more of a violation of privacy. Besides, he checked out."

"He checked out?"

"Oh boy," I said, pacing and thinking.

"Is that bad?" she said, looking worried.

"It could be. If you can't tell me where he's from, could you at least nod or shake your head if I get the state right?"

"I suppose it's not like I'm giving you his home address."

"Was he from New York?"

She nodded.

CHAPTER 36 – KATIE/FIXER

TRUE TO HER word, the reporter at The Gossip Zone forwarded a copy of the article that was hitting magazine's website at six o'clock. Minutes after, it would be shared across all social media. I clicked on the link she sent me and almost spit out the iced tea I was drinking when reading the first headline:

THOMAS EDWIN XAVIER ADMITS TO KIDNAPPING WOMAN CAUGHT ON VIDEO

Thomas Edwin Xavier, the founder of a TEX Security Contractors, LLC has been caught on video admitting to the kidnapping and harboring of a Massachusetts woman, which could torpedo any possible political future.

Now rivals, trying to stop his potential run for the office of the presidency, are in an all-out race to obtain the recorded admission hoping to publicize it, TGZ has learned.

After hearing news of the alleged kidnapping, TGZ searched through the archives. Is this another case like the many lawsuits Xavier has been through before? No comment from Thomas Xavier but stay tuned for more...

A second headline followed:

HOW WILL SECRET SEX LIFE OF THOMAS EDWIN XAVIER IMPACT POSSIBLE PRESIDENTIAL CAMPAIGN

To go along with the headlined article, the reporter put together a full page of photographs showing Xavier with three different women who unwittingly took part in his sexual proclivities, posed in various BDSM displays. The women's faces and body parts are blacked out to protect their identities.

Can Xavier keep his sexual bondage addiction at bay to run for the highest office of the land? Voters want to know: How many women were forced to sign NDAs for fear of retaliation?

My stomach started churning. This was it. Once those headlines made the rounds on the social media and were repeatedly shared by users, all hell was going to break loose. I had to be ready for Xavier's reaction. If past performance was any sign, the word would spread like wildfire on Instagram and Twitter. He might not observe social media religiously, but even if he didn't see it on the internet, the odds were pretty good it would make it to the mainstream. I wouldn't doubt if *Fox News* has their feelers watching Twitter looking for headlines. *CNN* was currently going through a staffing change, but they still kept their eyes peeled too. And *Telegram* was another popular avenue where information made the rounds.

With things in motion, I needed to head back and meet up with Sheriff Chase. If things moved as fast as I assume they would, the two of us needed to be ready to move.

I packed up everything and loaded it all into the duffel bag. I wasn't leaving anything behind for the time being. Once I shrugged on my bomber jacket and checked my weapon, I slipped the backpack over my shoulders. The white powder probably was no longer necessary; things were coming down to the wire. Then I slipped the key card into my pocket, grabbed my keys, and headed to the sheriff's station.

And prayed that my scheme didn't get May killed.

CHAPTER 37 - KATIE

SHERIFF CHASE AND I sat at the desk inside her office, monitoring the social media posts, watching for any that might appear to be Xavier. Once the articles went live and the reporter spent the next thirty minutes posting to all the tabloid's media accounts, we saw an uptick in likes, comments, and shares. Calls were coming in from citizen journalists and mainstream media reporters asking questions, wanting to know who had possession of the video in the headline.

The sheriff was monitoring Facebook, YouTube, and Instagram. I observed Twitter, TikTok, and Telegram.

Opposition research teams for the potential opponents in the presidential race were pushing for answers too.

Then we got the call we'd been waiting for. The goal was to get Thomas Edwin Xavier's attention. Once the TGZ reporter called to tell me he made contact; that was the signal for the next step. I expected he would threaten to sue, and order her to take the articles down. He also sent a text with a cease and desist letter attached.

We knew he was riled up. He kept calling her and screaming like he was having a histrionic meltdown. While the Sheriff prepared all the gear, I made the phone call.

I opened the burner phone that was left for me at the manager's office. Opened up the call logs and dialed the number.

"Where the hell have you been, Cole?" Xavier screamed into the phone the minute he picked up.

I placed my hand over the phone and looked at the sheriff. "He doesn't know his man is dead."

"Use that," she responded.

"I'm afraid Cole can't come to the phone right now," I said to Xavier, trying to keep my voice calm.

"Who the hell is this?"

"This is the PI you wanted Cole to kill."

I could hear the catch in his breath. "Where's Cole?"

"Like I said, he can't come to the phone. Now listen up: I've got something you want, and you've got something I want."

The phone went silent, but I could still hear him breathing. "I don't know what you're talking about."

"I want May!"

"You seem to be under the delusion that I have this person," he scoffed. "But even if I did, what makes you think I'd give her to you?"

"Oh, I think you will. You will release her into my custody, or I will start releasing face-time videos of you and your lackeys wherein you entered a conspiracy to commit murder, murder, and the potential blackmail of a United States Senator."

"You have no such thing," he said defiantly.

"Oh, no?" I pushed the play button on the video portion I re-recorded on my phone to use for just this purpose:

"The Sheriff is a small-town mentality who thinks this was about a burglary. As far as you know, she knows nothing about the photographs. And don't concern yourself about the woman. She's already being handled."

245

"What does that mean? She's being handled how?"

"It means she's in my possession, so there's no need to worry about her. Just take care of our current problem, then I can go public with my announcement for office and you'll get your last payment, and as agreed, a bonus for your discretion."

"Just in case it isn't clear, Mr. Xavier, I have it all: the photographs and every face-time recording where you gave your paid thugs the order of what to do."

"What's your intention with them?" he hissed.

"I think I made myself clear. I'm willing to give you the recordings, but only if you release May into my custody, alive and unharmed."

I could hear his evil smirk over the phone. "Why should I trust you?"

"Don't trust me then," I said, taking a chance he wouldn't hang up on me right then. "I'll just start releasing them and let the chips fall where they will."

"I can ruin the senator and have May deported," he said, which I expected to hear.

"Again, go ahead. Hal Colson is prepared to step down if he needs to. If you attempt to deport May, these videos will ruin you. I will not only release them, but give them to law enforcement. Are you prepared to give up everything?"

He got quiet again.

"How do I know you won't bring law enforcement?"

"You said yourself she's a small-town sheriff," I said, winking at Sheriff Chase, "do you really think her small department could go up against you? This is between you and me. I'm doing it for Mackie."

246

"Mackie," he smirked. "If those three would have minded their own business, we wouldn't be here now."

I didn't want to piss him off and ruin the plan, but that got my ire up. "Fact check: if you weren't a frigging pervert who got off on abusing women, those three men wouldn't have had to. Let's be clear; your dangerous fetish got us here."

I could hear his breathing escalate, and several seconds passed before he spoke again.

"If I agree with this, we meet alone. Just you and me. I come to Whispering Oak. That motel you're staying at is fine. I've checked it out."

I bet you have, I thought to myself. He wanted to keep it contained in the small town, where there was one female sheriff and a low level newspaper, instead of the jurisdiction of the NYPD and nosey reporters.

"I give you May," he continued. "You give me the phone with the videos. Then we're done."

"Once I have May, I'm out," I said, stunned that my voice was so calm. "How long will it take you to get here?"

"I can be there by morning," he responded.

"I'm in room eleven... and I meant what I said; May better be alive and unharmed."

"May is fine!"

"Prove it. Put her on the phone and ask her what she was wearing when she was abducted."

"Ridiculous, I'm not doing that."

"Then enjoy the next tabloid headlines."

He sighed in frustration. "Hold on."

I heard him walking. If he was at his main house on Lloyd Harbor, it was a large home, and who knew which part of the house he was keeping her? After several minutes of him huffing and puffing in aggravation, I heard a door open.

"What were you wearing when you were abducted?" I heard his voice say from a distance, as if he was holding the phone away.

"What?" I barely heard the female voice. It was so soft it was almost like a whisper, and I could tell she was scared. "Tell her what you were wearing when you were taken."

"A black Adidas athletic suit," she stuttered.

I heard the door close and then his walking again.

I gave thumbs up to Sheriff Chase, a signal to let her know Xavier just confirmed he still had May.

"I'll see you at seven a.m. tomorrow morning," he said, suddenly in a hurry to hang up.

"Do. Not. Hurt. Her.," I said, forcefully.

He was scowling when I disconnected from the call. I put my head in my hands, overwhelmed by it all, but also terrified he wouldn't stick to his end of the bargain, and harm May in an angry outburst.

"You know he's not coming alone, right?" Sheriff Chase said, rubbing my shoulder to let me know we were in this together.

I lifted my head up and nodded. "But he wants to do it, drawing no attention. What are the odds you got that DNA back on the blood you found in room twelve from our mysterious guest who was stabbed?"

She shook her head. "DNA takes a while, let alone this small urban town."

"Dammit, why didn't I think to get his license plate?"

"You couldn't have known that a guest at the motel was involved. Besides, the truck might not be his."

"But I should have suspected. His involvement makes little sense."

"What do you mean?"

"Why would he intervene when the two thugs entered my room and get one thug arrested, only to impersonate an attorney to provide him with cyanide? Why not just kill him in the room? He had a gun."

"Are you saying he didn't supply the cyanide?"

I shook my head, confused. "Do we know for certain that he did? Could the prisoner have hidden a capsule somewhere that Boyd wouldn't have checked when searching his pockets?"

Sheriff Chase snorted. "Sounds like you're getting into conspiracy theories now."

I gave her a half-nod, but kept quiet. There was something about the situation that just wasn't sitting right with me. But then again, maybe it was a simple case of not wanting to share in the last payment. He wanted the bonus for himself.

"We're almost there, Katie," she said. "Don't second guess things now."

I grabbed my phone. "I guess we've got some calls to make and things to do to get ready."

"That we do."

CHAPTER 38 – KATIE

SHERIFF CHASE WAS on the department phone making calls while I made calls from my cell phone. After we set things in motion, we finished up so we could both head out and try to get some sleep. She got side-tracked helping Deputy Boyd handle some of the evidence from the blue van, so I walked outside alone. The minute I did, I got the feeling I was being watched, but also acknowledged that it could be the stress.

Discreetly, I checked the surroundings, looked up and down the street, and verified there weren't any vehicles parked nearby that shouldn't be there. Instinctively, I was looking for the Ford truck, but knew he wouldn't park it where I might see it. Xavier could still try to have me killed, thinking I kept the evidence in my possession. If I was out of the way, he could keep May and, in his view, the evidence would disappear. I kept my right hand on my gun, until I stepped into the SUV, and then I removed it from the holster and placed it on my lap.

The sheriff was right. I was the bait in this charade. I knew better than to think it couldn't all go sideways. Xavier thought he had knowledge on his side. He viewed Sheriff Chase as a small-town cop with no resources, and I was a PI with less than six months at the job, at that. He was probably feeling rather cocky.

I pulled into the motel parking lot. No cars. The office light was off, the sign on the door to ring the bell. The yellow tape was finally off of room twelve.

That trick wouldn't work twice, so I parked and entered room eleven, with the gun firmly in my hand. I locked and chained it once I was inside, and verified there were no visitors.

The gun was still in my hand, so I set it down on the desk. I slipped off the bomber jacket and gun holster, hung them on the rack, and then dropped the backpack on the chair. The only thing I had to look forward to was the leftover turkey pot pie from the diner. I pulled it out of the small refrigerator, took the aluminum lid off, and nuked it. The waitress supplied me with plastic utensils and napkins. After two minutes, I removed it from the microwave and sat down on the edge of the bed to enjoy what could be my last meal.

CHAPTER 39 – KATIE/FIXER

"BLACKY CHEVY SUBURBAN driving down Main Street," a male voice said into the earpiece in my ear. "I make out one male driver, one male passenger in front, tinted windows in back."

I glanced at the time on my watch for the umpteenth time. "Looks like Xavier lied. He didn't come alone, but at least he's on time."

After several hours of trying to sleep, I finally gave up. I dragged the chair over toward the back of the room, so that it faced the door. All of my belongings were locked up in the SUV. All I had with me was my gun, the photographs, and the cell phone.

I had been sitting in the chair for two hours now; too nervous to do anything else. Just waiting. I jumped at every noise. I got up when one noise was close by and peered out through the curtains. It was dark out, but it looked like a deputy was escorting the motel manager into his vehicle and leaving the premises. Good, one person who wouldn't be in danger. I pulled the curtains to the side, even the sheers, to let the sunlight in when it showed up through the early morning fog.

"The vehicle is pulling into the lot now," the voice said in my ear.

"Just you and me," I said to anyone listening.

"Two bodyguards stepped out of the vehicle. Guns out, they're searching the perimeter."

My hands were sweaty, my nerves raw.

"Back door is opening. Thomas Edwin Xavier is coming out. Hold on… he's leaning into the vehicle.

Affirmative. The woman is with him. I repeat, he has the woman."

I stood up now with my gun ready.

"All four of them are headed toward the room."

My heart was pounding a mile a minute. I was afraid if I didn't calm down, I would give myself a heart attack. I took a deep breath. Held it, and let it out. And repeated the calming process two more times.

"Somebody entering the room now."

I could visibly see the door being pushed open. I purposely kept it open about an inch, so I wouldn't have to walk over when they arrived.

I saw a gun, and then the face of the man holding it. It wasn't Xavier. It was one of his men.

"I'm just checking the room for other players," he said, seeing me with my weapon.

"And yet, Xavier brought you," I said, pointing out the hypocrisy.

The bodyguard did a quick sweep, checked the bathroom, and shower, and under the beds. I had my gun trained on him the entire time.

Once he verified the room was empty, except for the terrified female; me, he exited the room.

"The two bodyguards are getting into position outside the door," I heard in the earpiece.

At least he was coming in alone. I stood a better chance with one on one than me against the three of them.

I braced myself when the door opened again. The woman was pushed through first. He slipped inside and kept his body behind her, but a gun was pointed toward me just over her shoulder on the right. Coward. He was using her as a shield. I studied her face. She looked terrified, but thankfully, I didn't notice bruises and the abuse I feared I would see.

"Are you okay, May?"

He nudged her in the back. In response, she nodded, but didn't speak. He coached her.

"Give me the photos and phone," he demanded.

"Not so fast," I said, trying to look into the cowardly eyes of the man who ordered the hit on Mackie. I held the items in my left hand up so that he could see. "Let May go and I'll put them on the desk at the same time."

He said nothing for a minute, but then he positioned himself toward the desk so that they'd be in an easy reach of his hand.

He nudged her to move at the same time I eased my left hand forward. I dropped the photographs and phone on the desk, grabbed May's arm, and pulled her behind me.

He snatched them up, and the two of us faced off. My gun was pointed directly at his head; his toward mine, too. My jaw clenched, the anger flooding through my body and into my brain, over what this man put so many people through. He didn't deserve to live, let alone campaign for the highest office of the land. He thought I was just a novice PI, but what he didn't know was that Finn worked tirelessly with me at his obstacle course and at the shooting range. I might not have Xavier's skill level, but I could pull the trigger just as well as he could when my life was on the line. But with the help of Finn and Derek, I was also getting smart.

"Looks like we have a stand-off," I said.

His eyes turned dark, which didn't match his sudden smile. "You didn't think I would trust you when you said that you'd walk away after this, did you?"

I shrugged, trying to show that I wasn't rattled. "Not any more than you saying you'd come alone," I said with just as much mirth in my voice.

"This is how I see it, Katie," he said with a smirk. "I was a soldier, trained to kill. And I was good at it, which is why my security firm became so successful. I bet your experience with that gun is shooting at targets at a controlled gun range. You've been at this PI gig for what, months at the most?"

I knew as I stared into the eyes of this man that he intended to kill me.

"I agree. I'm pretty new at this stuff and it doesn't look good for me," I said, keeping my voice steady.

"I have to commend you for trying though," he said, and his smile almost looked pleasant there for a minute. "You put up a good fight."

"I gave it my best," I said, keeping my eyes alert, watching the movement of his finger, but it wasn't on the trigger. Something was going on.

"But I can't let May go," he finally said.

And then I heard a sound and noticed a peripheral movement out of the corner of my left eye. I kept my eyes on Xavier. But now he was wearing a genuine smile.

"We've got movement inside the room," a voice said through the earpiece. "Holy shit!"

And then it was like some zombie movie, and a figure rose out of the mattress. The bedspread was thrown to the side. Heath, the man from room nine, sat straight up inside a square space that had been cut out of the mattress. The gun in his hand was aimed at me.

My eyes darted back and forth between the two of them. If I took my gun off of Xavier, he'd shoot. No matter which one I aimed at, one of them would shoot. Xavier had me.

"Now, if you would, please return May to me."

I heard her scream, but in my stunned reaction, it sounded like it was further away. She latched on to my arms, and her nails dug into my skin. She was terrified of going back with him, and I knew what he would to do her, if she did. I had to make a quick decision.

"Okay," I said, moving slightly as if I was ready to return May. "I'm ready."

And then I squeezed the trigger. The bullet fractured the smile right off Xavier's face as he slumped to the floor. Simultaneously, a bullet shattered the motel window and Heath's brain matter was splattered all over the bed.

Shaking from adrenaline, I saw Sheriff Chase standing outside the window. Seconds later, her face was filled with relief as she dropped the gun into a plastic evidence bag being held by Deputy Boyd. She was involved in an officer-involved shooting.

My body felt a chill as the reality set in that I was forced to kill a man at close range. I slipped my gun back into my holster, and then wrapped my arms around May, who was screaming and crying uncontrollably.

"Sheriff, they're both down," I said into the radio.

Within a few seconds, Sheriff Chase and Deputy Boyd were inside the room, escorting us out. On the way, I grabbed the evidence that fell from Xavier's hands. It wouldn't be needed for a trial, since all three players were dead, but we made a promise to a journalist. It would be up to the sheriff to deal with the two bodyguards to find out if they had any knowledge.

"This is what happens when a man thinks he's dealing with two novices from small-town USA," Sheriff Chase said once we were out in the fresh air.

She had called in for mutual aid. The Springfield State Police had the place cordoned off, and the bodyguards were in custody. The locals were standing out on the sidewalk, watching, and clapping, because the people who killed two locals were taken down. But I saw a familiar face; Derek was in the crowd. When he saw me looking, he smiled and gave me a nod—his way of saying he had my back—and then slipped into the back of his SUV, and his driver stepped on the gas.

I pulled myself away from May, opened the back of my SUV and retrieved my cell phone. I punched in the number to the burner phone I gave Sierra. When she picked up, her voice sounded anxious, as expected.

"I have somebody who wants to speak with you," I said, and then I handed the phone to May.

"Hello," May said tentatively into the phone, not knowing who it was.

Her face lit up with a smile when she heard Sierra's voice on the other end. She started crying again, but they were tears of joy. "Sierra, it is so good to hear your voice?"

I walked over to Sheriff Chase. "I have to ask; how did you know the guy was in the mattress?"

"When the troopers did a sweep of the streets, they found his Ford truck," she said. "So we knew he was in the room, just not where. Then Boyd threw it out as a hypothetical."

"Hang on to him. That man is wicked smart."

"Thing is," she continued. "We think he planned to do that before you set up the meeting with Xavier. He was hired to kill and get the evidence either way."

I shivered at the thought. *How long had he been there?* I didn't sleep on the second bed, so didn't give it a second thought.

"I can't thank you enough for your help with this," I said sincerely.

She scoffed. "To hell with that. You helped me. I wouldn't have been able to handle this without your help. I'm grateful Mackie called you in."

I smiled.

"I found some things in the blue van we confiscated. The rest of what we found is in the evidence lock-up, for now, but I thought you should have these right away."

She handed me a small box. I opened it to see the medals that were stolen, along with the note my dad wrote when he gave Mackie his Silver Star. When I looked back up at the sheriff, my eyes were filled with tears. I hugged her, even though I could tell she wasn't the hugging type.

"Thank you."

EPILOGUE

I STAYED IN Whispering Oak for two more days to attend Mackie's funeral. Hal showed up and thanked me profusely for what I did for May. He informed me he was retiring from his senate seat. That he knew eventually the story would come out regarding his involvement, so he wanted to own up to it.

After the procession, I joined the locals at the diner to say our own farewell. Sheriff Chase and I exchanged numbers and agreed to visit each other. She had never been to Cape Cod, so I said she had an open invitation when the renovations on my cottage were completed.

"So what's up for you now?" she said on the way to my car.

I thought about it for a moment. "I think I'm going to do what I can to help May stay here permanently, without hiding in the shadows.

She smiled and handed me a business card. "Somehow, I thought you might say that. He's an attorney in New York who handles immigration issues. There is a special victim's law that you might look into for asylum."

"I'll definitely call him," I said.

"Again, thank you, Katie," she said. "You can come and consult with us anytime."

I slipped behind the wheel as she walked away and joined her other deputies. I waved on the way out of the parking lot. For now, I was headed back to reality.

I sent a text to Olivia and Madison, filling them in on what happened, and reminded them to call me when their cruise ship pulled into port. Finn could no longer accept calls since he went dark. I would just have to wait for him to reach out. Then I sent a text to Derek.

"Tell Bailey I'm coming home."

CR HIATT writes action-oriented stories with strong female characters, some psychological suspense, and a touch of romance. When she's not writing, doing research or investigating, she's usually renovating houses, riding her e-bike and spending time outdoors with her Golden Retriever, daughter, and friends, usually somewhere near the water.

Dear Readers:

Thank you for purchasing and reading Warriors She Knew. Readers and word of mouth are crucial to an author's success. If you read the book and enjoyed it, I would be honored if you would consider leaving a one or two-line review on Amazon.

Thank you so much.

For more information on CR HIATT:
https://www.facebook.com/CRHIATT

Also, feel free to email me to receive updates:
authorCRHIATT@gmail.com.

Made in the USA
Middletown, DE
16 August 2023